Penguin Popular Classics

Macbeth

BY WILLIAM SHAKESPEARE

PENGUIN POPULAR CLASSICS

MACBETH

WILLIAM SHAKESPEARE

PENGUIN BOOKS

PENGUIN BOOKS

Published by the Penguin Group
Penguin Books Ltd, 80 Strand, London WC2R ORL, England
Penguin Putnam Inc., 375 Hudson Street, New York, New York 10014, USA
Penguin Books Australia Ltd, Ringwood, Victoria, Australia
Penguin Books Canada Ltd, 10 Alcorn Avenue, Toronto, Ontario, Canada M4V 3B2
Penguin Books India (P) Ltd, 11 Community Centre, Panchsheel Park,
New Delhi – 110 017, India
Penguin Books (NZ) Ltd, Cnr Rosedale and Airborne Roads, Albany, Auckland,
New Zealand
Penguin Books (South Africa) (Pty) Ltd, 24 Sturdee Avenue, Rosebank 2196, South Africa

Penguin Books Ltd, Registered Offices: 80 Strand, London WC2R ORL, England

www.penguin.com

Published in Penguin Popular Classics 1994
28

Copyright 1934 by the Estate of G. B. Harrison

Printed in England by Cox & Wyman Ltd, Reading, Berkshire

CONTENTS

THE WORKS OF SHAKESPEARE

WILLIAM SHAKESPEARE

William Shakespeare was born at Stratford upon Avon in April, 1564. He was the third child, and eldest son, of John Shakespeare and Mary Arden. His father was one of the most prosperous men of Stratford, who held in turn the chief offices in the town. His mother was of gentle birth, the daughter of Robert Arden of Wilmcote. In December, 1582, Shakespeare married Ann Hathaway, daughter of a farmer of Shottery, near Stratford; their first child Susanna was baptized on May 6, 1583, and twins, Hamnet and Judith, on February 22, 1585. Little is known of Shakespeare's early life; but it is unlikely that a writer who dramatized such an incomparable range and variety of human kinds and experiences should have spent his early manhood entirely in placid pursuits in a country town. There is one tradition, not universally accepted, that he fled from Stratford because he was in trouble for deer stealing, and had fallen foul of Sir Thomas Lucy, the local magnate; another that he was for some time a schoolmaster.

From 1592 onwards the records are much fuller. In March, 1592, the Lord Strange's players produced a new play at the Rose Theatre called *Harry the Sixth*, which was very successful, and was probably the *First Part of Henry VI*. In the autumn of 1592 Robert Greene, the best known of the professional writers, as he was dying wrote a letter to three fellow writers in which he warned them against the ingratitude of players in general, and in particular against an 'upstart crow' who 'supposes he is as much able to bombast out a blank verse as the best of you: and being an absolute Johannes Factotum is in his own conceit the only

Shake-scene in a country.' This is the first reference to Shakespeare and the whole passage suggests that Shakespeare had become suddenly famous as a playwright. At this time Shakespeare was brought into touch with Edward Alleyne the great tragedian, and Christopher Marlowe, whose thundering parts of Tamburlaine, the Jew of Malta, and Dr Faustus Alleyne was acting, as well as Hieronimo, the hero of Kyd's *Spanish Tragedy*, the most famous of all Elizabethan plays.

In April, 1593, Shakespeare published his poem *Venus and Adonis*, which was dedicated to the young Earl of Southampton: it was a great and lasting success, and was reprinted nine times in the next few years. In May, 1594, his second poem, *The Rape of Lucrece*, was also dedicated to Southampton.

There was little playing in 1593, for the theatres were shut during a severe outbreak of the plague; but in the autumn of 1594, when the plague ceased, the playing companies were reorganized, and Shakespeare became a sharer in the Lord Chamberlain's company who went to play in the Theatre in Shoreditch. During these months Marlowe and Kyd had died. Shakespeare was thus for a time without a rival. He had already written the three parts of *Henry VI*, *Richard III*, *Titus Andronicus*, *The Two Gentlemen of Verona*, *Love's Labour's Lost*, *The Comedy of Errors*, and *The Taming of the Shrew*. Soon afterwards he wrote the first of his greater plays – *Romeo and Juliet* – and he followed this success in the next three years with *A Midsummer Night's Dream*, *Richard II*, and *The Merchant of Venice*. The two parts of *Henry IV*, introducing Falstaff, the most popular of all his comic characters, were written in 1597–8.

The company left the Theatre in 1597 owing to disputes over a renewal of the ground lease, and went to play at the

Curtain in the same neighbourhood. The disputes continued throughout 1598, and at Christmas the players settled
the matter by demolishing the old Theatre and re-erecting
a new playhouse on the South bank of the Thames, near
Southwark Cathedral. This playhouse was named the
Globe. The expenses of the new building were shared by
the chief members of the Company, including Shakespeare,
who was now a man of some means. In 1596 he had bought
New Place, a large house in the centre of Stratford, for £60,
and through his father purchased a coat-of-arms from the
Heralds, which was the official recognition that he and his
family were gentlefolk.

By the summer of 1598 Shakespeare was recognized as
the greatest of English dramatists. Booksellers were print-
ing his more popular plays, at times even in pirated or stolen
versions, and he received a remarkable tribute from a young
writer named Francis Meres, in his book *Palladis Tamia*. In
a long catalogue of English authors Meres gave Shakespeare
more prominence than any other writer, and mentioned by
name twelve of his plays.

Shortly before the Globe was opened Shakespeare had
completed the cycle of plays dealing with the whole story
of the Wars of the Roses with *Henry V*. It was followed by
As You Like it, and *Julius Caesar*, the first of the maturer
tragedies. In the next three years he wrote *Troylus and
Cressida*, *The Merry Wives of Windsor*, *Hamlet* and *Twelfth
Night*.

On March 24, 1603, Queen Elizabeth died. The company
had often performed before her, but they found her suc-
cessor a far more enthusiastic patron. One of the first acts
of King James was to take over the company and to pro-
mote them to be his own servants, so that henceforward
they were known as the King's Men. They acted now very

frequently at Court, and prospered accordingly. In the early years of the reign Shakespeare wrote the more sombre comedies, *All's Well that Ends Well*, and *Measure for Measure*, which were followed by *Othello*, *Macbeth* and *King Lear*. Then he returned to Roman themes with *Antony and Cleopatra* and *Coriolanus*.

Since 1601 Shakespeare had been writing less, and there were now a number of rival dramatists who were introducing new styles of drama, particularly Ben Jonson (whose first successful comedy, *Every Man in his Humour*, was acted by Shakespeare's company in 1598), Chapman, Dekker, Marston, and Beaumont and Fletcher who began to write in 1607. In 1608 the King's Men acquired a second playhouse, an indoor private theatre in the fashionable quarter of the Blackfriars. At private theatres, plays were performed indoors; the prices charged were higher than in the public playhouses, and the audience consequently was more select. Shakespeare seems to have retired from the stage about this time: his name does not occur in the various lists of players after 1607. Henceforward he lived for the most part at Stratford, where he was regarded as one of the most important citizens. He still wrote a few plays, and he tried his hand at the new form of tragi-comedy – a play with tragic incidents but a happy ending – which Beaumont and Fletcher had popularized. He wrote four of these – *Pericles*, *Cymbeline*, *The Winter's Tale* and *The Tempest*, which was acetd at Court in 1611. For the last four years of his life he lived in retirement. His son Hamnet had died in 1596: his two daughters were now married. Shakespeare died at Stratford upon Avon on April 23, 1616, and was buried in the chancel of the church, before the high altar. Shortly afterwards a memorial which still exists, with a portrait bust, was set up on the North wall. His wife survived him.

When Shakespeare died fourteen of his plays had been published separately in Quarto booklets. In 1623 his surviving fellow actors, John Heming and Henry Condell, with the co-operation of a number of printers, published a collected edition of thirty-six plays in one Folio volume, with an engraved portrait, memorial verses by Ben Jonson and others, and an Epistle to the Reader in which Heming and Condell make the interesting note that Shakespeare's 'hand and mind went together, and what he thought, he uttered with that easiness that we have scarce received from him a blot in his papers'.

The plays as printed in the Quartos or the Folio differ considerably from the usual modern text. They are often not divided into scenes, and sometimes not even into acts. Nor are there place-headings at the beginning of each scene, because in the Elizabethan theatre there was no scenery. They are carelessly printed and the spelling is erratic.

THE ELIZABETHAN THEATRE

Although plays of one sort and another had been acted for many generations, no permanent playhouse was erected in England until 1576. In the 1570's the Lord Mayor and Aldermen of the City of London and the players were constantly at variance. As a result James Burbage, then the leader of the great Earl of Leicester's players, decided that he would erect a playhouse outside the jurisdiction of the Lord Mayor, where the players would no longer be hindered by the authorities. Accordingly in 1576 he built the Theatre in Shoreditch, at that time a suburb of London. The experiment was successful, and by 1592 there were two more playhouses in London, the Curtain (also in Shoreditch), and the Rose on the south bank of the river, near Southwark Cathedral.

Elizabethan players were accustomed to act on a variety of stages; in the great hall of a nobleman's house, or one of the Queen's palaces, in town halls and in yards, as well as their own theatre.

The public playhouse for which most of Shakespeare's plays were written was a small and intimate affair. The outside measurement of the Fortune Theatre, which was built in 1600 to rival the new Globe, was but eighty feet square. Playhouses were usually circular or octagonal, with three tiers of galleries looking down upon the yard or pit, which was open to the sky. The stage jutted out into the yard so that the actors came forward into the midst of their audience.

Over the stage there was a roof, and on either side doors by which the characters entered or disappeared. Over the back of the stage ran a gallery or upper stage which was used whenever an upper scene was needed, as when Romeo climbs up to Juliet's bedroom, or the citizens of Angiers address King John from the walls. The space beneath this upper stage was known as the tiring house; it was concealed from the audience by a curtain which would be drawn back to reveal an inner stage, for such scenes as the witches' cave in *Macbeth*, Prospero's cell, or Juliet's tomb.

There was no general curtain concealing the whole stage, so that all scenes on the main stage began with an entrance and ended with an exit. Thus in tragedies the dead must be carried away. There was no scenery, and therefore no limit to the number of scenes, for a scene came to an end when the characters left the stage. When it was necessary for the exact locality of a scene to be known, then Shakespeare

THE GLOBE THEATRE

Wood-engraving by R. J. Beedham after a reconstruction by J. C. Adams

indicated it in the dialogue; otherwise a simple property or a garment was sufficient; a chair or stool showed an indoor scene, a man wearing riding boots was a messenger, a king wearing armour was on the battlefield, or the like. Such simplicity was on the whole an advantage; the spectator was not distracted by the setting and Shakespeare was able to use as many scenes as he wished. The action passed by very quickly: a play of 2500 lines of verse could be acted in two hours. Moreover, since the actor was so close to his audience, the slightest subtlety of voice and gesture was easily appreciated.

The company was a 'Fellowship of Players', who were all partners and sharers. There were usually ten to fifteen full members, with three or four boys, and some paid servants. Shakespeare had therefore to write for his team. The chief actor in the company was Richard Burbage, who first distinguished himself as Richard III; for him Shakespeare wrote his great tragic parts. An important member of the company was the clown or low comedian. From 1594 to 1600 the company's clown was Will Kemp; he was succeeded by Robert Armin. No women were allowed to appear on the stage, and all women's parts were taken by boys.

THE TRAGEDY OF MACBETH

In *The Tragedy of Macbeth* Shakespeare dramatized certain events and legends of the history of Scotland in the eleventh century recorded in Ralph Holinshed's *Chronicles,* from which he borrowed and altered freely. Holinshed told how Macbeth's imaginations were first fired by the prophecies of 'three women in strange and wild apparel, resembling creatures of the elder world'. Egged on by the importunity of his wife, Macbeth slew Duncan, with the aid of Banquo and other friends. Holinshed gave no details of the murder of Duncan. This episode Shakespeare adapted from the murder of King Duff by Donwald, who also was encouraged by an ambitious wife. Duff is portrayed in the woodcut in the *Chronicle* as an old warrior with an ample white beard. According to Holinshed Macbeth at first was a good king and made admirable laws, but after some years, remembering the words of the Weird Sisters, he began to fear that he would, in his own turn, be murdered. Accordingly Banquo was slain, but Fleance, his son, escaped and became the ancestor of the House of Stuart. The *Chronicle* does not, however, record any appearance of Banquo's ghost. Macbeth's character now degenerated, and, warned by a prophecy, he began to suspect Macduff; but a certain witch 'told that he should never be slain with man born of any woman, nor vanquished till the wood of Bernane came to the Castle of Dunsinane'.

When Macduff fled, Macbeth came tô his Castle, which was unsuspectingly opened to him, and caused Macduff's wife, children and people to be murdered. Macduff took refuge in England and came to Malcolm, and their long conversation was closely reproduced in Act IV, Scene 3. After this there was a general revolt against Macbeth. When Macduff reached Bernane wood he ordered his men to cut down boughs to cover their advance against Dunsinane Castle. Macbeth led his men out, though he perceived that the first warning prophecy was now fulfilled, but when he saw the great numbers of Macduff's army he fled away on horseback. Macduff pursued him and brought him to bay. Macbeth cried that he was not appointed to be slain by any creature that is born of woman. Macduff replied, '"It is true, Macbeth, and now shall thine insatiable cruelty have an end, for I am even he that thy wizards have told thee of; who was never born of my mother, but ripped out of her womb." Therewithal he stept unto him, and slew him in the place. Then cutting his head from his shoulders, he set it upon a pole, and brought it unto Malcolm.'

The play was probably written in 1606. The style, and especially the teeming poetic imagery of the great speeches, belong rather to the period of *Lear* (1606) than of *Hamlet* (1601). Moreover, the remarks of the Porter (p. 49 ll. 16–19) – 'Faith here's an equivocator, that could swear in both the scales against either scale, who committed treason enough for God's sake yet could not equivocate to Heaven' – are a likely reference to the notorious trial of Father Garnet on March 28, 1606, for complicity in the Gunpowder Plot. Garnet admitted in his defence that he had deliberately deceived his accusers, and justified himself by the Jesuit doctrine of equivocation (see note on p. 49 ll. 16–19 on p. 114–115).

Although the great scenes in *Macbeth* – the murder of Duncan, the banquet, the sleepwalking – are unsurpassed anywhere, *Macbeth* is in some ways the least satisfactory of Shakespeare's mature tragedies. The last Act falls away, and there are several patches of verse very inferior to the rest. Most editors have agreed that the play was partly revised after Shakespeare had written it. The speech of the 'bleeding Captain', if not the whole of Act I, Scene 2, and the operatic episodes of Hecate and the witches (Act III, Scene 5, and Act IV, Scene 1) are not in Shakespeare's manner, and Thomas Middleton, who wrote a play called *The Witch*, about 1612, is generally credited, or debited, with them. The songs, to which reference is made in the stage directions of the Hecate scenes, are given in full in *The Witch*.

There is some external evidence of revision. Simon Forman, a notorious quack and astrologer, kept notes of some plays which he saw in 1611. Of *Macbeth* at the Globe, on April 20 he wrote – 'There was to be obserued, firste, howe Mackbeth and Bancko, 2 noble men of Scotland, Ridinge thorowe a wod, the(re) stode before them 3 women feiries or Nimphes, And saluted Mackbeth, sayinge, 3 tyms vnto him, haille Mackbeth, king of Codon; for thou shalt be a kinge, but shalt beget No kinges, &c. Then said Bancko, What all to Mackbeth And nothing to me. Yes, said the nimphes, haille to thee Bancko, thou shalt beget kinges, yet be no kinge. And so they departed & cam to the Courte of Scotland to Dunkin king of Scotes, and yt was in the dais of Edward the Confessor. And Dunkin bad them both kindly wellcome, And made Mackbeth forth with Prince of Northumberland, and sent him hom to his own castell, and appointed Mackbeth to prouid for him, for he would sup with him the next dai at night, & did soe. And Mackbeth contriued to kill Dunkin, & thorowe the persuasion of his wife did that

night Murder the kinge in his own Castell, beinge his
guest. And ther were many prodigies seen that night &
the dai before. And when Mack Beth had murdered the
kinge, the blod on his handes could not be washed of by
Any meanes, nor from his wiues handes, which handled
the bloddi daggers in hiding them, By which means
they became both moch amazed & Affronted. The
murder being knowen, Dunkins 2 sonns fled, the on to
England, the [other to] Walles, to saue them selues, they
being fled, they were supposed guilty of the murder of
their father, which was nothinge so. Then was Mackbeth
crowned kinge, and then he for feare of Banko, his old
companion, that he should beget kinges but be no kinge
him selfe, he contriued the death of Banko, and caused
him to be Murdred on the way as he Rode. The next
night, being at supper with his noble men whom he had
bid to a feaste to the which also Banco should haue com,
he began to speake of Noble Banco, and to wish that he
wer ther. And as he thus did, standing vp to drincke a
Carouse to him, the ghoste of Banco came and sate down
in his cheier behind him. And he turninge About to sit
down Again sawe the goste of Banco, which fronted him
so, that he fell into a great passion of fear and fury, Vtter-
ynge many wordes about his murder, by which, when
they hard that Banco was Murdred they Suspected
Mackbet.

'Then MackDove fled to England to the kinges sonn,
And soe they Raised an Army, And cam into Scotland,
and at Dunston Anyse overthrue Mackbet. In the mean-
tyme whille Macdouee was in England, Mackbet slewe
Mackdoues wife & children, and after in the battelle
Mackdoue slewe Mackbet.

'Obserue Also howe Mackbetes quen did Rise in the

night in her slepe, & walke and talked and confessed all,
& the docter noted her wordes.'

[Quoted in E. K. Chambers' *William Shakespeare*, ii,
337–8.]

There is no trace, in the play as now known, of any
episode where the blood on the hands of Macbeth and his
wife could not be washed off, nor is it a confused memory
of the sleepwalking scene.

There are several other indications in the text that either
Shakespeare was himself revising or rewriting an older
play, or, more probably, that he had a collaborator. These
are most noticeable in the last Act, particularly in scenes
2, 6 and 8, where the rhythms are unlike Shakespeare's
and the rhymes are unusually feeble. The difference
between Shakespeare's usual style and the inferior work
can be seen by comparing two small scenes, linking up
the main action. In Act II Scene 4 the conversation between Ross and the old man is not in the style of Shakespeare, who seldom invented such a turgid phrase as 'dark
night strangles the travelling lamp'. On the other hand,
in Act III Scene 6 Lennox's speech is, by contrast, full of
the subtlest tones and hints of meaning. At times the join
where Shakespeare's verse is patched on to inferior work
is almost perceptible. The speech (p. 101 l. 29) beginning
'If thou speak'st false . . .' begins in Shakespeare's style
down to

> 'I pull in resolution, and begin
> To doubt th' equivocation of the fiend,
> That lies like truth. Fear not, till Birnam wood
> Do come to Dunsinane;'

Then the solemn rhythm changes pace, and proceeds at a
rapid trot –

'Arm, arm, and out,
If this which he avouches, does appear,
There is nor flying hence, nor tarrying here,
I 'gin to be aweary of the sun,
And wish th' estate o' th' world were now undone.
Ring the alarum-bell, blow wind, come wrack,
At least we'll die with harness on our back.'

If, as is likely, these inconsistencies of style are due to
hasty writing, then a probable occasion of the play was the
visit of King Christian of Denmark, King James's brother-
in-law, to the English Court from 17th July to 14th
August, 1606. Shakespeare and his company were the
King's Players, and it was a natural occasion for them to
produce a story of Scottish History touching on the
ancestry of their patron. In the previous summer, when
King James made a visit in state to the University of Ox-
ford, three small boys dressed like nymphs greeted him
with a short Latin dialogue reminding him of the ancient
legend of the Three Sisters who had prophesied the future
glories of Banquo's descendants. Now, as before in other
plays intended for the Court – *A Midsummer Night's Dream*
and *The Merry Wives of Windsor* – Shakespeare worked in
some compliment to the royal audience, such as the vision
of the eight kings seen by Macbeth (p. 79), or the tactful
reference to King James's divine touch in healing those
afflicted by the King's Evil. There was no time to polish
the play, for the King of Denmark arrived somewhat un-
expectedly, so that Shakespeare worked on the high
scenes, leaving the last Act but sketched out and ill-
proportioned, the minor characters imperfect and slightly
drawn, and trusting to an assistant to fill in the gaps.
It was a common practice for dramatists to collaborate,

especially when, for any reason, a play was needed in a hurry.

This is, admittedly, a hypothesis, but some explanation of the inconsistency in *Macbeth* is necessary. I suggest therefore that *Macbeth* was written in haste by Shakespeare and Another, who was responsible for the Bleeding Captain, the Old Man, and much of Act V; some years later the play was revised for another Court performance, and the witch scenes, as they now exist, substituted by Middleton for those in the original play.

Macbeth was first printed in the First Folio in 1623; there is no earlier text. The text in the Folio is, on the whole, accurately printed, apparently from a fair copy made for stage use. It has certain peculiarities. Capital letters are used lavishly, and in several passages the division of the verse lines is apparently incorrect. Editors have endeavoured to set the verse lines right, but not always very successfully, for many verse lines in the play were not written in the formal five stress metre, but in a free rhythmic verse.

The punctuation of the Folio text differs from modern usage. The modern custom is to punctuate according to syntax, the Elizabethan to punctuate for recitation. The Folio text divides the play into Acts and Scenes, but gives no place headings; these have been added by editors of the eighteenth and nineteenth centuries.

Indeed, the 'authorized text' of Shakespeare differs considerably from the Folio. A modern editor is therefore in difficulty. If he reprints exactly the Folio text with all its antique spellings and inconsistent punctuation he will confuse and irritate the general reader; if he simply follows the 'authorized text' he will annoy those who have studied the recent work of scholars. I have therefore compromised, and the present text may best be described as the Folio text, conservatively modernized. The spelling is modernized, but the original punctuation and arrangement have been kept except in places where they seemed obviously wrong. The reader who is used to the 'authorised text' may find the text, at first sight, unfamiliar, but it is nearer to Shakespeare's own version, and to the play as presented by his actors.

The Tragedy of
Macbeth

THE ACTORS' NAMES

DUNCAN, King of Scotland

MALCOLM
DONALBAIN } his sons

MACBETH
BANQUO } generals of the King's army

MACDUFF
LENNOX
ROSS
MENTEITH } noblemen of Scotland
ANGUS
CAITHNESS

FLEANCE, son to Banquo

SIWARD, Earl of Northumberland, general of the English
forces

Young SIWARD, his son

SEYTON, an officer attending on Macbeth

Boy, son to Macduff

An English Doctor

A Scottish Doctor

A Captain

A Soldier

A Porter

An Old Man

Three murderers

LADY MACBETH

LADY MACDUFF

Gentlewoman attending on Lady Macbeth

HECATE

Three Witches

Apparitions

Lords, Gentlemen, Officers, Soldiers, Attendants, and Messengers

I.1

Thunder and lightning. Enter three Witches.

FIRST WITCH: When shall we three meet again?
In thunder, lightning, or in rain?

SECOND WITCH: When the hurly-burly's done,
When the battle's lost, and won.

THIRD WITCH: That will be ere the set of sun.

FIRST WITCH: Where the place?

SECOND WITCH: Upon the Heath.

THIRD WITCH: There to meet with Macbeth.

FIRST WITCH: I come, Graymalkin.

ALL: Paddock calls anon:
Fair is foul, and foul is fair,
Hover through the fog and filthy air.
Exeunt.

I.2

Alarum within. Enter King Duncan, Malcolm, Donalbain,
Lennox, with Attendants, meeting a bleeding Captain.

DUNCAN: What bloody man is that? He can report,
As seemeth by his plight, of the revolt
The newest state.

MALCOLM: This is the Sergeant,
Who like a good and hardy soldier fought
'Gainst my captivity: hail brave friend;
Say to the King, the knowledge of the broil,
As thou didst leave it.

CAPTAIN: Doubtful it stood,

As two spent swimmers, that do cling together,
And choke their art. The merciless Macdonwald
(Worthy to be a rebel, for to that
The multiplying villanies of Nature
Do swarm upon him) from the Western Isles
Of kerns and gallowglasses is suppli'd,
And Fortune on his damned quarry smiling,
Show'd like a rebel's whore: but all's too weak:
For brave Macbeth (well he deserves that name)
Disdaining Fortune, with his brandish'd steel,
Which smok'd with bloody execution,
(Like Valour's minion) carv'd out his passage,
Till he fac'd the slave:
Which ne'er shook hands, nor bade farewell to him,
Till he unseam'd him from the nave to th' chops,
And fix'd his head upon our battlements.

DUNCAN: O valiant cousin, worthy gentleman.

CAPTAIN: As whence the sun 'gins his reflection,
Shipwracking storms, and direful thunders break:
So from that spring, whence comfort seem'd to come,
Discomfort swells. Mark King of Scotland, mark,
No sooner Justice had, with Valour arm'd,
Compell'd these skipping kerns to trust their heels,
But the Norweyan Lord, surveying vantage,
With furbish'd arms, and new supplies of men,
Began a fresh assault.

DUNCAN: Dismay'd not this our Captains, Macbeth and
Banquo?

CAPTAIN: Yes, as sparrows eagles; or the hare the lion:
If I say sooth, I must report they were
As cannons overcharg'd with double cracks,
So they doubly redoubled strokes upon the foe:
Except they meant to bathe in reeking wounds,

Or memorize another Golgotha,
I cannot tell: but I am faint,
My gashes cry for help.
DUNCAN: So well thy words become thee, as thy wounds,
They smack of honour both: go get him surgeons.

Enter Ross and Angus.

Who comes here?
MALCOLM: The worthy Thane of Ross.
LENNOX: What a haste looks through his eyes!
So should he look, that seems to speak things strange.
ROSS: God save the King.
DUNCAN: Whence cam'st thou, worthy Thane?
ROSS: From Fife, great King,
Where the Norweyan banners flout the sky,
And fan our people cold.
Norway himself, with terrible numbers,
Assisted by that most disloyal traitor,
The Thane of Cawdor, began a dismal conflict,
Till that Bellona's bridegroom, lapp'd in proof,
Confronted him with self-comparisons,
Point against point, rebellious arm 'gainst arm,
Curbing his lavish spirit: and to conclude,
The victory fell on us.
DUNCAN: Great happiness.
ROSS: That now Sweno, the Norways' King,
Craves composition:
Nor would we deign him burial of his men,
Till he disbursed, at Saint Colme's Inch,
Ten thousand dollars, to our general use.
DUNCAN: No more that Thane of Cawdor shall deceive
Our bosom interest: go pronounce his present death,

And with his former title greet Macbeth.
ROSS: I'll see it done.
DUNCAN: What he hath lost, noble Macbeth hath won.

Exeunt.

I. 3

Thunder. Enter the three Witches.

FIRST WITCH: Where hast thou been, sister?
SECOND WITCH: Killing swine.
THIRD WITCH: Sister, where thou?
FIRST WITCH: A sailor's wife had chestnuts in her lap,
   And mounch'd, and mounch'd, and mounch'd:
   Give me, quoth I.
   Aroint thee, witch, the rump-fed ronyon cries.
   Her husband's to Aleppo gone, Master o' th' *Tiger*:
   But in a sieve I'll thither sail,
   And like a rat without a tail,
   I'll do, I'll do, and I'll do.
SECOND WITCH: I'll give thee a wind.
FIRST WITCH: Th' art kind.
THIRD WITCH: And I another.
FIRST WITCH: I myself have all the other,
   And the very ports they blow,
   All the quarters that they know,
   I' th' shipman's card.
   I 'll drain him dry as hay:
   Sleep shall neither night nor day
   Hang upon his pent-house lid:
   He shall live a man forbid:
   Weary sev'nights, nine times nine,
   Shall he dwindle, peak, and pine:

Though his bark cannot be lost,
Yet it shall be tempest-tost.
Look what I have.

SECOND WITCH: Show me, show me.

FIRST WITCH: Here I have a pilot's thumb,
Wrack'd, as homeward he did come.

Drum within.

THIRD WITCH: A drum, a drum:
Macbeth doth come.

ALL: The Weird Sisters, hand in hand,
Posters of the sea and land,
Thus do go, about, about,
Thrice to thine, and thrice to mine,
And thrice again, to make up nine.
Peace, the charm's wound up.

Enter Macbeth and Banquo.

MACBETH: So foul and fair a day I have not seen.

BANQUO: How far is't call'd to Forres? What are these,
So wither'd, and so wild in their attire,
That look not like th' inhabitants o' th' earth,
And yet are on't? Live you, or are you aught
That man may question? You seem to understand me,
By each at once her choppy finger laying
Upon her skinny lips: you should be women,
And yet your beards forbid me to interpret
That you are so.

MACBETH: Speak if you can: what are you?

FIRST WITCH: All hail Macbeth, hail to thee Thane of
Glamis.

SECOND WITCH: All hail Macbeth, hail to thee Thane of
Cawdor.

THIRD WITCH: All hail Macbeth, that shalt be King
hereafter.

BANQUO: Good sir, why do you start, and seem to fear
  Things that do sound so fair? I' th' name of truth
  Are ye fantastical, or that indeed
  Which outwardly ye show? My noble partner
  You greet with present grace, and great prediction
  Of noble having, and of royal hope,
  That he seems rapt withal: to me you speak not.
  If you can look into the seeds of Time,
  And say, which grain will grow, and which will not,
  Speak then to me, who neither beg, nor fear
  Your favours, nor your hate.

FIRST WITCH: Hail.

SECOND WITCH: Hail.

THIRD WITCH: Hail.

FIRST WITCH: Lesser than Macbeth, and greater.

SECOND WITCH: Not so happy, yet much happier.

THIRD WITCH: Thou shalt get Kings, though thou be
    none:
  So all hail Macbeth, and Banquo.

FIRST WITCH: Banquo, and Macbeth, all hail.

MACBETH: Stay you imperfect speakers, tell me more:
  By Sinel's death, I know I am Thane of Glamis,
  But how, of Cawdor? the Thane of Cawdor lives
  A prosperous gentleman: and to be King,
  Stands not within the prospect of belief,
  No more than to be Cawdor. Say from whence
  You owe this strange intelligence, or why
  Upon this blasted Heath you stop our way
  With such prophetic greeting?
  Speak, I charge you.

                    Witches vanish.

BANQUO: The earth hath bubbles, as the water has,
  And these are of them: whither are they vanish'd?

MACBETH: Into the air: and what seem'd corporal,
Melted, as breath into the wind.
Would they had stay'd.
BANQUO: Were such things here, as we do speak about?
Or have we eaten on the insane root,
That takes the reason prisoner?
MACBETH: Your children shall be Kings.
BANQUO: You shall be King.
MACBETH: And Thane of Cawdor too: went it not so?
BANQUO: To th' selfsame tune, and words: who's here?
Enter Ross and Angus.
ROSS: The King hath happily receiv'd, Macbeth,
The news of thy success: and when he reads
Thy personal venture in the rebels' fight,
His wonders and his praises do contend,
Which should be thine, or his: silenc'd with that,
In viewing o'er the rest o' th' selfsame day,
He finds thee in the stout Norweyan ranks,
Nothing afeard of what thyself didst make
Strange images of death. As thick as tale
Came post with post, and every one did bear
Thy praises in his Kingdom's great defence,
And pour'd them down before him.
ANGUS: We are sent,
To give thee from our Royal Master thanks,
Only to herald thee into his sight,
Not pay thee.
ROSS: And for an earnest of a greater honour,
He bade me, from him, call thee Thane of Cawdor:
In which addition, hail most worthy Thane,
For it is thine.
BANQUO: What, can the Devil speak true?
MACBETH: The Thane of Cawdor lives:

Why do you dress me in borrowed robes?

ANGUS: Who was the Thane, lives yet,
But under heavy judgement bears that life,
Which he deserves to lose.
Whether he was combin'd with those of Norway,
Or did line the rebel with hidden help,
And vantage; or that with both he labour'd
In his country's wrack, I know not:
But treasons capital, confess'd, and prov'd,
Have overthrown him.

MACBETH: Glamis, and Thane of Cawdor:
The greatest is behind. Thanks for your pains.
Do you not hope your children shall be Kings,
When those that gave the Thane of Cawdor to me,
Promis'd no less to them?

BANQUO: That trusted home,
Might yet enkindle you unto the Crown,
Besides the Thane of Cawdor. But 'tis strange:
And oftentimes, to win us to our harm,
The instruments of darkness tell us truths,
Win us with honest trifles, to betray's
In deepest consequence.
Cousins, a word, I pray you.

MACBETH: Two truths are told,
As happy Prologues to the swelling Act
Of the imperial theme. I thank you gentlemen:
This supernatural soliciting
Cannot be ill; cannot be good.
If ill? why hath it given me earnest of success,
Commencing in a truth? I am Thane of Cawdor.
If good? why do I yield to that suggestion,
Whose horrid image doth unfix my hair,
And make my seated heart knock at my ribs,

Against the use of Nature? Present fears
Are less than horrible imaginings:
My thought, whose murther yet is but fantastical,
Shakes so my single state of man,
That function is smother'd in surmise,
And nothing is, but what is not.

BANQUO: Look how our partner's rapt.

MACBETH: If Chance will have me King,
Why Chance may crown me,
Without my stir.

BANQUO: New honours come upon him
Like our strange garments, cleave not to their mould,
But with the aid of use.

MACBETH: Come what come may,
Time, and the hour, runs through the roughest day.

BANQUO: Worthy Macbeth, we stay upon your leisure.

MACBETH: Give me your favour:
My dull brain was wrought with things forgotten.
Kind gentlemen, your pains are register'd,
Where every day I turn the leaf,
To read them.
Let us toward the King: think upon
What hath chanc'd: and at more time,
The interim having weigh'd it, let us speak
Our free hearts each to other.

BANQUO: Very gladly.

MACBETH: Till then enough:
Come friends.

Exeunt.

Flourish. Enter King Duncan, Lennox, Malcolm, Donalbain,
and Attendants.

DUNCAN: Is execution done on Cawdor?
Are not those in commission yet return'd?

MALCOLM: My Liege, they are not yet come back.
But I have spoke with one that saw him die:
Who did report, that very frankly he
Confess'd his treasons, implor'd you Highness' pardon,
And set forth a deep repentance:
Nothing in his life became him,
Like the leaving it. He died,
As one that had been studied in his death,
To throw away the dearest thing he ow'd,
As 'twere a careless trifle.

DUNCAN: There's no art,
To find the mind's construction in the face.
He was a gentleman, on whom I built
An absolute trust.

> *Enter Macbeth, Banquo, Ross, and Angus.*

O worthiest cousin,
The sin of my ingratitude even now
Was heavy on me. Thou art so far before,
That swiftest wing of recompense is slow,
To overtake thee. Would thou hadst less deserv'd,
That the proportion both of thanks, and payment,
Might have been mine: only I have left to say,
More is thy due, than more than all can pay.

MACBETH: The service, and the loyalty I owe,
In doing it, pays itself.
Your Highness' part, is to receive our duties:

And our duties are to your throne, and state,
Children, and servants; which do but what they should,
By doing every thing safe toward your love
And honour.
DUNCAN: Welcome hither:
I have begun to plant thee, and will labour
To make thee full of growing. Noble Banquo,
That hast no less deserv'd, nor must be known
No less to have done so: let me enfold thee,
And hold thee to my heart.
BANQUO: There if I grow,
The harvest is your own.
DUNCAN: My plenteous joys,
Wanton in fulness, seek to hide themselves
In drops of sorrow. Sons, kinsmen, Thanes,
And you whose places are the nearest, know,
We will establish our estate upon
Our eldest, Malcolm, whom we name hereafter,
The Prince of Cumberland: which honour must
Not unaccompanied, invest him only,
But signs of nobleness, like stars, shall shine
On all deservers. From hence to Inverness,
And bind us further to you.
MACBETH: The rest is labour, which is not us'd for you:
I'll be myself the harbinger, and make joyful
The hearing of my wife, with your approach:
So humbly take my leave.
DUNCAN: My worthy Cawdor.
MACBETH: The Prince of Cumberland: that is a step,
On which I must fall down, or else o'erleap,
For in my way it lies. Stars hide your fires,
Let not light see my black and deep desires:
The eye wink at the hand; yet let that be,

Which the eye fears, when it is done to see.

Exit.

DUNCAN: True, worthy Banquo: he is full so valiant,
And in his commendations, I am fed:
It is a banquet to me. Let's after him,
Whose care is gone before, to bid us welcome:
It is a peerless kinsman.

Flourish. Exeunt.

I. 5

Enter Macbeth's wife alone with a letter.

LADY MACBETH: *They met me in the day of success: and I
have learn'd by the perfect'st report, they have more in them,
than mortal knowledge. When I burnt in desire to question
them further, they made themselves air, into which they
vanish'd. Whiles I stood rapt in the wonder of it, came
missives from the King, who all-hail'd me Thane of Cawdor,
by which title before, these Weird Sisters saluted me, and
referr'd me to the coming on of time, with hail King that
shalt be. This have I thought good to deliver thee (my dearest
partner of greatness) that thou mightst not lose the dues of
rejoicing by being ignorant of what greatness is promis'd thee.
Lay it to thy heart and farewell.*

Glamis thou art, and Cawdor, and shalt be
What thou art promis'd: yet do I fear thy nature,
It is too full o' th' milk of humane kindness,
To catch the nearest way. Thou wouldst be great,
Art not without ambition, but without
The illness should attend it. What thou wouldst highly,
That wouldst thou holily: wouldst not play false,
And yet wouldst wrongly win.

Thou 'ldst have, great Glamis, that which cries,
Thus thou must do, if thou have it;
And that which rather thou dost fear to do,
Than wishest should be undone. Hie thee hither,
That I may pour my spirits in thine ear,
And chastise with the valour of my tongue
All that impedes thee from the golden round,
Which Fate and metaphysical aid doth seem
To have thee crown'd withal.

Enter Messenger.

What is your tidings?

MESSENGER: The King comes here to-night.

LADY MACBETH: Thou 'rt mad to say it.
Is not thy Master with him? who, were't so,
Would have inform'd for preparation.

MESSENGER: So please you, it is true: our Thane is
coming:
One of my fellows had the speed of him;
Who almost dead for breath, had scarcely more
Than would make up his message.

LADY MACBETH: Give him tending,
He brings great news.

Exit Messenger.

The raven himself is hoarse,
That croaks the fatal entrance of Duncan
Under my battlements. Come you spirits,
That tend on mortal thoughts, unsex me here,
And fill me from the crown to the toe, top-full
Of direst cruelty: make thick my blood,
Stop up th' access and passage to remorse,
That no compunctious visitings of Nature
Shake my fell purpose, nor keep peace between
Th' effect, and it. Come to my woman's breasts,

And take my milk for gall, you murth'ring ministers,
Wherever, in your sightless substances,
You wait on Nature's mischief. Come thick Night,
And pall thee in the dunnest smoke of Hell,
That my keen knife see not the wound it makes,
Nor Heaven peep through the blanket of the dark,
To cry, hold, hold.

Enter Macbeth.

Great Glamis, worthy Cawdor,
Greater than both, by the all-hail hereafter,
Thy letters have transported me beyond
This ignorant present, and I feel now
The future in the instant.

MACBETH: My dearest love,
Duncan comes here to-night.

LADY MACBETH: And when goes hence?

MACBETH: To-morrow, as he purposes.

LADY MACBETH: O never,
Shall sun that morrow see.
Your face, my Thane, is as a book, where men
May read strange matters: to beguile the time,
Look like the time, bear welcome in your eye,
Your hand, your tongue: look like th' innocent flower,
But be the serpent under 't. He that's coming,
Must be provided for: and you shall put
This night's great business into my dispatch,
Which shall to all our nights, and days to come,
Give solely sovereign sway, and masterdom.

MACBETH: We will speak further.

LADY MACBETH: Only look up clear:
To alter favour, ever is to fear:
Leave all the rest to me.

Exeunt.

I. 6

Oboes, and torches. Enter King Duncan, Malcolm, Donalbain,
Banquo, Lennox, Macduff, Ross, Angus, and Attendants.

DUNCAN: This Castle hath a pleasant seat,
The air nimbly and sweetly recommends itself
Unto our gentle senses.

BANQUO: This guest of summer,
The temple-haunting martlet does approve,
By this loved mansionry, that the Heaven's breath
Smells wooingly here: no jutty frieze,
Buttress, nor coign of vantage, but this bird
Hath made his pendent bed, and procreant cradle:
Where they most breed, and haunt, I have observ'd
The air is delicate.

Enter Lady Macbeth.

DUNCAN: See, see our honour'd hostess:
The love that follows us, sometime is our trouble,
Which still we thank as love. Herein I teach you,
How you shall bid God 'ild us for your pains,
And thank us for your trouble.

LADY MACBETH: All our service,
In every point twice done, and then done double,
Were poor, and single business, to contend
Against those honours deep, and broad,
Wherewith your Majesty loads our House:
For those of old, and the late dignities,
Heap'd up to them, we rest your hermits.

DUNCAN: Where's the Thane of Cawdor?
We cours'd him at the heels, and had a purpose
To be his purveyor: but he rides well,
And his great love (sharp as his spur) hath holp him

To his home before us: fair and noble hostess
We are your guest to-night.
LADY MACBETH: Your servants ever,
Have theirs, themselves, and what is theirs in compt,
To make their audit at your Highness' pleasure,
Still to return your own.
DUNCAN: Give me your hand:
Conduct me to mine host: we love him highly,
And shall continue our graces towards him.
By your leave hostess.

Exeunt.

I.7

*Oboes. Torches. Enter a Sewer, and divers Servants with dishes
and service over the stage. Then enter Macbeth.*
MACBETH: If it were done, when 'tis done, then 'twere
well,
It were done quickly: if th' assassination
Could trammel up the consequence, and catch
With his surcease, success: that but this blow
Might be the be-all, and the end-all. Here,
But here, upon this bank and school of time,
We'ld jump the life to come. But in these cases,
We still have judgement here, that we but teach
Bloody instructions, which being taught, return
To plague th' inventor. This even-handed Justice
Commends th' ingredients of our poison'd chalice
To our own lips. He's here in double trust;
First, as I am his kinsman, and his subject,
Strong both against the deed: then, as his host,
Who should against his murtherer shut the door,

Not bear the knife myself. Besides, this Duncan
Hath borne his faculties so meek; hath been
So clear in his great office, that his virtues
Will plead like angels, trumpet-tongu'd against
The deep damnation of his taking-off:
And Pity, like a naked new-born babe,
Striding the blast, or Heaven's cherubin, hors'd
Upon the sightless couriers of the air,
Shall blow the horrid deed in every eye,
That tears shall drown the wind. I have no spur
To prick the sides of my intent, but only
Vaulting Ambition, which o'erleaps itself,
And falls on th' other.

Enter Lady Macbeth.

How now? What news?

LADY MACBETH: He has almost supp'd: why have you
    left the chamber?

MACBETH: Hath he ask'd for me?

LADY MACBETH: Know you not, he has?

MACBETH: We will proceed no further in this business:
He hath honour'd me of late, and I have bought
Golden opinions from all sorts of people,
Which would be worn now in their newest gloss,
Not cast aside so soon.

LADY MACBETH: Was the hope drunk,
Wherein you dress'd yourself? Hath it slept since?
And wakes it now to look so green, and pale,
At what it did so freely? From this time,
Such I account thy love. Art thou afear'd
To be the same in thine own act, and valour,
As thou art in desire? Wouldst thou have that
Which thou esteem'st the ornament of life,
And live a coward in thine own esteem?

Letting I dare not, wait upon I would,
Like the poor cat i' th' adage.

MACBETH: Prithee peace:
I dare do all that may become a man,
Who dares do more, is none.

LADY MACBETH: What beast was't then
That made you break this enterprise to me?
When you durst do it, then you were a man:
And to be more than what you were, you would
Be so much more the man. Nor time, nor place
Did then adhere, and yet you would make both:
They have made themselves, and that their fitness now
Does unmake you. I have given suck, and know
How tender 'tis to love the babe that milks me:
I would, while it was smiling in my face,
Have pluck'd my nipple from his boneless gums,
And dash'd the brains out, had I so sworn
As you have done to this.

MACBETH: If we should fail?

LADY MACBETH: We fail?
But screw your courage to the sticking-place,
And we'll not fail: when Duncan is asleep,
(Whereto the rather shall his day's hard journey
Soundly invite him) his two chamberlains
Will I with wine, and wassail, so convince,
That memory, the warder of the brain,
Shall be a fume, and the receipt of reason
A limbeck only: when in swinish sleep,
Their drenched natures lie as in a death,
What cannot you and I perform upon
Th' unguarded Duncan? What not put upon
His spongy officers? who shall bear the guilt
Of our great quell.

MACBETH: Bring forth men-children only:
For thy undaunted mettle should compose
Nothing but males. Will it not be receiv'd,
When we have mark'd with blood those sleepy two
Of his own chamber, and us'd their very daggers,
That they have done 't?

LADY MACBETH: Who dares receive it other,
As we shall make our griefs and clamour roar,
Upon his death?

MACBETH: I am settled, and bend up
Each corporal agent to this terrible feat.
Away, and mock the time with fairest show,
False face must hide what the false heart doth know.

Exeunt.

II. 1

Enter Banquo, and Fleance, with a torch before him.

BANQUO: How goes the night, boy?

FLEANCE: The moon is down: I have not heard the clock.

BANQUO: And she goes down at twelve.

FLEANCE: I take 't, 'tis later, sir.

BANQUO: Hold, take my sword:
There's husbandry in Heaven,
Their candles are all out: take thee that too.
A heavy summons lies like lead upon me,
And yet I would not sleep:
Powers, restrain in me the cursed thoughts
That Nature gives way to in repose.

Enter Macbeth, and a Servant with a torch.

Give me my sword: who's there?

MACBETH: A friend.

BANQUO: What sir, not yet at rest? The King's a-bed.
He hath been in unusual pleasure,
And sent forth great largess to your offices.
This diamond he greets your wife withal,
By the name of most kind hostess,
And shut up in measureless content.

MACBETH: Being unprepar'd,
Our will became the servant to defect,
Which else should free have wrought.

BANQUO: All's well.
I dreamt last night of the three Weird Sisters:
To you they have show'd some truth.

MACBETH: I think not of them:
Yet when we can entreat an hour to serve,
We would spend it in some words upon that business,
If you would grant the time.

BANQUO: At your kind'st leisure.

MACBETH: If you shall cleave to my consent,
When 'tis, it shall make honour for you.

BANQUO: So I lose none,
In seeking to augment it, but still keep
My bosom franchis'd, and allegiance clear,
I shall be counsell'd.

MACBETH: Good repose the while.

BANQUO: Thanks sir: the like to you.

Exeunt Banquo and Fleance.

MACBETH: Go bid thy Mistress, when my drink is ready,
She strike upon the bell. Get thee to bed.

Exit Servant.

Is this a dagger, which I see before me,
The handle toward my hand? Come, let me clutch
thee:
I have thee not, and yet I see thee still.

Art thou not, fatal vision, sensible
To feeling, as to sight? or art thou but
A dagger of the mind, a false creation,
Proceeding from the heat-oppressed brain?
I see thee yet, in form as palpable,
As this which now I draw.
Thou marshall'st me the way that I was going,
And such an instrument I was to use.
Mine eyes are made the fools o' th' other senses,
Or else worth all the rest: I see thee still;
And on thy blade, and dudgeon, gouts of blood,
Which was not so before. There's no such thing:
It is the bloody business, which informs
Thus to mine eyes. Now o'er the one half-world
Nature seems dead, and wicked dreams abuse
The curtain'd sleep: witchcraft celebrates
Pale Hecat's offerings: and wither'd Murther,
Alarum'd by his sentinel, the wolf,
Whose howl's his watch, thus with his stealthy pace,
With Tarquin's ravishing strides, towards his design
Moves like a ghost. Thou sure and firm-set Earth
Hear not my steps, which way they walk, for fear
Thy very stones prate of my whereabout,
And take the present horror from the time,
Which now suits with it. Whiles I threat, he lives:
Words to the heat of deeds too cold breath gives.
                    A bell rings.
I go, and it is done: the bell invites me.
Hear it not, Duncan, for it is a knell,
That summons thee to Heaven, or to Hell.
                    Exit.

II. 2

Enter Lady Macbeth.

LADY MACBETH: That which hath made them drunk, hath
 made me bold:
What hath quench'd them, hath given me fire.
Hark, peace: it was the owl that shriek'd,
The fatal bellman, which gives the stern'st good-night.
He is about it, the doors are open:
And the surfeited grooms do mock their charge
With snores. I have drugg'd their possets,
That Death and Nature do contend about them,
Whether they live, or die.

Enter Macbeth.

MACBETH: Who's there? what hoa?

LADY MACBETH: Alack, I am afraid they have awak'd,
And 'tis not done: th' attempt, and not the deed,
Confounds us: hark: I laid their daggers ready,
He could not miss 'em. Had he not resembled
My father as he slept, I had done't.
My husband!

MACBETH: I have done the deed:
Didst thou not hear a noise?

LADY MACBETH: I heard the owl scream, and the crickets
 cry.
Did not you speak?

MACBETH: When?

LADY MACBETH: Now.

MACBETH: As I descended?

LADY MACBETH: Ay.

MACBETH: Hark, who lies i' th' second chamber?

LADY MACBETH: Donalbain.

MACBETH: This is a sorry sight.

LADY MACBETH: A foolish thought, to say a sorry sight.

MACBETH: There's one did laugh in's sleep,
  And one cried Murther, that they did wake each other:
  I stood, and heard them: but they did say their prayers,
  And address'd them again to sleep.

LADY MACBETH: There are two lodg'd together.

MACBETH: One cried God bless us, and Amen the other,
  As they had seen me with these hangman's hands:
  Listening their fear, I could not say Amen,
  When they did say God bless us.

LADY MACBETH: Consider it not so deeply.

MACBETH: But wherefore could not I pronounce Amen?
  I had most need of blessing, and Amen stuck in my throat.

LADY MACBETH: These deeds must not be thought
  After these ways: so, it will make us mad.

MACBETH: Methought I heard a voice cry, Sleep no more:
  Macbeth does murther Sleep, the innocent Sleep,
  Sleep that knits up the ravell'd sleave of care,
  The death of each day's life, sore labour's bath,
  Balm of hurt minds, great Nature's second course,
  Chief nourisher in Life's feast.

LADY MACBETH: What do you mean?

MACBETH: Still it cri'd, Sleep no more to all the House:
  Glamis hath murther'd Sleep, and therefore Cawdor
  Shall sleep no more: Macbeth shall sleep no more.

LADY MACBETH: Who was it, that thus cried? Why
    worthy Thane,
  You do unbend your noble strength, to think
  So brain-sickly of things: go get some water,
  And wash this filthy witness from your hand.
  Why did you bring these daggers from the place?
  They must lie there: go carry them, and smear

The sleepy grooms with blood.

MACBETH: I'll go no more:
I am afraid, to think what I have done:
Look on't again, I dare not.

LADY MACBETH: Infirm of purpose:
Give me the daggers: the sleeping, and the dead,
Are but as pictures: 'tis the eye of childhood,
That fears a painted devil. If he do bleed,
I'll gild the faces of the grooms withal,
For it must seem their guilt.

Exit. Knock within.

MACBETH: Whence is that knocking?
How is't with me, when every noise appals me?
What hands are here? hah: they pluck out mine eyes.
Will all great Neptune's Ocean wash this blood
Clean from my hand? No: this my hand will rather
The multitudinous seas incarnadine,
Making the green one, red.

Enter Lady Macbeth.

LADY MACBETH: My hands are of your colour: but I shame
To wear a heart so white.

Knock.

I hear a knocking at the south entry:
Retire we to our chamber:
A little water clears us of this deed.
How easy is it then? Your constancy
Hath left you unattended.

Knock.

Hark, more knocking.
Get on your nightgown, lest occasion call us,
And show us to be watchers: be not lost
So poorly in your thoughts.

MACBETH: To know my deed,

Knock.

'Twere best not know myself.
Wake Duncan with thy knocking:
I would thou could'st.

Exeunt.

II. 3

Enter a Porter. Knocking within.

PORTER: Here's a knocking indeed: if a man were Porter of Hell Gate, he should have old turning the key. (*Knock.*) Knock, knock, knock. Who's there i' th' name of Beelzebub? Here's a farmer, that hang'd himself on th' expectation of plenty: come in time, have napkins enow about you, here you'll sweat for't. (*Knock.*) Knock, knock. Who's there in th' other Devil's name? Faith here's an equivocator, that could swear in both the scales against either scale, who committed treason enough for God's sake, yet could not equivocate to Heaven: oh come in, equivocator. (*Knock.*) Knock, knock, knock. Who's there? 'Faith here's an English tailor come hither, for stealing out of a French hose: come in tailor, here you may roast your goose. (*Knock.*) Knock, knock. Never at quiet: what are you? But this place is too cold for Hell. I'll devil-porter it no further: I had thought to have let in some of all professions, that go the primrose way to th' everlasting bonfire. (*Knock.*) Anon, anon, I pray you remember the porter.

Enter Macduff, and Lennox.

MACDUFF: Was it so late, friend, ere you went to bed,
That you do lie so late?

PORTER: 'Faith sir, we were carousing till the second cock: and drink sir, is a great provoker of three things.

MACDUFF: What three things does drink especially provoke?

PORTER: Marry, sir, nose-painting, sleep, and urine. Lechery, sir, it provokes and unprovokes: it provokes the desire, but it takes away the performance. Therefore much drink may be said to be an equivocator with lechery: it makes him, and it mars him; it sets him on, and it takes him off; it persuades him, and disheartens him; makes him stand to, and not stand to: in conclusion, equivocates him in a sleep, and, giving him the lie, leaves him.

MACDUFF: I believe, drink gave thee the lie last night.

PORTER: That it did, sir, i' the very throat on me: but I requited him for his lie, and (I think) being too strong for him, though he took up my legs sometime, yet I made a shift to cast him.

Enter Macbeth.

MACDUFF: Is thy Master stirring?
Our knocking has awak'd him: here he comes.

LENNOX: Good morrow, noble sir.

MACBETH: Good morrow both.

MACDUFF: Is the King stirring, worthy Thane?

MACBETH: Not yet.

MACDUFF: He did command me to call timely on him;
I have almost slipp'd the hour.

MACBETH: I'll bring you to him.

MACDUFF: I know this is a joyful trouble to you:
But yet 'tis one.

MACBETH: The labour we delight in, physics pain:
This is the door.

MACDUFF: I'll make so bold to call, for 'tis my limited
   service.

Exit Macduff.

LENNOX: Goes the King hence to-day?

MACBETH: He does: he did appoint so.

LENNOX: The night has been unruly:
  Where we lay, our chimneys were blown down,
  And (as they say) lamentings heard i' th' air;
  Strange screams of death,
  And prophesying, with accents terrible,
  Of dire combustion, and confus'd events,
  New hatch'd to th' woeful time.
  The obscure bird clamour'd the livelong night.
  Some say, the earth was feverous,
  And did shake.

MACBETH: 'Twas a rough night.

LENNOX: My young remembrance cannot parallel
  A fellow to it.

Enter Macduff.

MACDUFF: O horror, horror, horror,
  Tongue nor heart cannot conceive, nor name thee.

MACBETH AND LENNOX: What's the matter?

MACDUFF: Confusion now hath made his masterpiece:
  Most sacrilegious murther hath broke ope
  The Lord's anointed Temple, and stole thence
  The life o' th' building.

MACBETH: What is't you say, the life?

LENNOX: Mean you his Majesty?

MACDUFF: Approach the chamber, and destroy your sight
  With a new Gorgon. Do not bid me speak:
  See, and then speak yourselves: awake, awake,

      Exeunt Macbeth and Lennox.

Ring the alarum-bell: murther, and treason,

Banquo, and Donalbain: Malcolm awake,
Shake off this downy sleep, Death's counterfeit,
And look on Death itself: up, up, and see
The great Doom's image: Malcolm, Banquo,
As from your graves rise up, and walk like sprites,
To countenance this horror. Ring the bell.

Bell rings. Enter Lady Macbeth.

LADY MACBETH: What's the business?
That such a hideous trumpet calls to parley
The sleepers of the House? speak, speak.

MACDUFF: O gentle Lady,
'Tis not for you to hear what I can speak:
The repetition in a woman's ear,
Would murther as it fell.

Enter Banquo.

O Banquo, Banquo, our Royal Master's murther'd.

LADY MACBETH: Woe, alas:
What, in our House?

BANQUO: Too cruel, any where.
Dear Duff, I prithee contradict thyself,
And say, it is not so.

Enter Macbeth, Lennox and Ross.

MACBETH: Had I but died an hour before this chance,
I had liv'd a blessed time: for from this instant,
There's nothing serious in mortality:
All is but toys: Renown and Grace is dead,
The wine of Life is drawn, and the mere lees
Is left this vault, to brag of.

Enter Malcolm and Donalbain.

DONALBAIN: What is amiss?

MACBETH: You are, and do not know't:
The spring, the head, the fountain of your blood
Is stopp'd, the very source of it is stopp'd.

MACDUFF: Your Royal Father's murther'd

MALCOLM: O, by whom?

LENNOX: Those of his chamber, as it seem'd, had done't:
Their hands and faces were all badg'd with blood,
So were their daggers, which unwip'd, we found
Upon their pillows: they star'd, and were distracted,
No man's life was to be trusted with them.

MACBETH: O, yet I do repent me of my fury,
That I did kill them.

MACDUFF: Wherefore did you so?

MACBETH: Who can be wise, amaz'd, temperate, and
furious,
Loyal, and neutral, in a moment? No man:
Th' expedition of my violent love
Outrun the pauser, Reason. Here lay Duncan,
His silver skin, lac'd with his golden blood,
And his gash'd stabs, look'd like a breach in Nature,
For Ruin's wasteful entrance: there the murtherers,
Steep'd in the colours of their trade; their daggers
Unmannerly breech'd with gore: who could refrain,
That had a heart to love; and in that heart
Courage, to make 's love known?

LADY MACBETH: Help me hence, hoa.

MACDUFF: Look to the Lady.

MALCOLM: Why do we hold our tongues,
That most may claim this argument for ours?

DONALBAIN: What should be spoken here,
Where our fate hid in an auger-hole,
May rush, and seize us? Let's away,
Our tears are not yet brew'd.

MALCOLM: Nor our strong sorrow
Upon the foot of motion.

BANQUO: Look to the Lady:

And when we have our naked frailties hid,
That suffer in exposure, let us meet,
And question this most bloody piece of work,
To know it further. Fears and scruples shake us:
In the great hand of God I stand, and thence,
Against the indivulg'd pretence, I fight
Of treasonous malice.

MACDUFF: And so do I.

ALL: So all.

MACBETH: Let's briefly put on manly readiness,
And meet i' th' Hall together.

ALL: Well contented.

Exeunt.

MALCOLM: What will you do?
Let's not consort with them:
To show an unfelt sorrow, is an office
Which the false man does easy.
I'll to England.

DONALBAIN: To Ireland I:
Our separated fortune shall keep us both the safer:
Where we are, there's daggers in men's smiles;
The near in blood, the nearer bloody.

MALCOLM: This murtherous shaft that's shot,
Hath not yet lighted: and our safest way,
Is to avoid the aim. Therefore to horse,
And let us not be dainty of leave-taking,
But shift away: there's warrant in that theft,
Which steals itself, when there's no mercy left.

Exeunt.

II. 4

Enter Ross, with an old Man.

OLD MAN: Threescore and ten I can remember well,
Within the volume of which time, I have seen
Hours dreadful, and things strange: but this sore night
Hath trifled former knowings.

ROSS: Ha, good father,
Thou seest the Heavens, as troubled with man's act,
Threatens his bloody stage: by th' clock 'tis day,
And yet dark Night strangles the travelling lamp:
Is't Night's predominance, or the Day's shame,
That Darkness does the face of Earth entomb,
When living Light should kiss it?

OLD MAN: 'Tis unnatural,
Even like the deed that's done: on Tuesday last,
A falcon towering in her pride of place,
Was by a mousing owl hawk'd at, and kill'd.

ROSS: And Duncan's horses,
(A thing most strange and certain)
Beauteous, and swift, the minions of their race,
Turn'd wild in nature, broke their stalls, flung out,
Contending 'gainst obedience, as they would
Make war with mankind.

OLD MAN: 'Tis said, they eat each other.

ROSS: They did so:
To th' amazement of mine eyes that look'd upon't.
Enter Macduff.
Here comes the good Macduff.
How goes the world sir, now?

MACDUFF: Why see you not?

ROSS: Is't known who did this more than bloody deed?

MACDUFF: Those that Macbeth hath slain.

ROSS: Alas the day,
  What good could they pretend?

MACDUFF: They were suborned:
  Malcolm and Donalbain, the King's two sons,
  Are stol'n away and fled, which puts upon them
  Suspicion of the deed.

ROSS: 'Gainst Nature still;
  Thriftless Ambition, that wilt ravin up
  Thine own life's means: then 'tis most like,
  The sovereignty will fall upon Macbeth.

MACDUFF: He is already nam'd, and gone to Scone
  To be invested.

ROSS: Where is Duncan's body?

MACDUFF: Carried to Colmekill,
  The sacred storehouse of his predecessors,
  And guardian of their bones.

ROSS: Will you to Scone?

MACDUFF: No cousin, I'll to Fife.

ROSS: Well, I will thither.

MACDUFF: Well may you see things well done there:
  adieu,
  Lest our old robes sit easier than our new.

ROSS: Farewell, father.

OLD MAN: God's benison go with you, and with those
  That would make good of bad, and friends of foes.

Exeunt omnes.

III. 1

Enter Banquo.

BANQUO: Thou hast it now, King, Cawdor, Glamis, all,
As the Weird Women promis'd, and I fear
Thou play'dst most foully for't: yet it was said
It should not stand in thy posterity,
But that myself should be the root, and father
Of many Kings. If there come truth from them,
As upon thee Macbeth, their speeches shine,
Why by the verities on thee made good,
May they not be my oracles as well,
And set me up in hope? But hush, no more.

Sennet sounded. Enter Macbeth as King, Lady Macbeth,
Lennox, Ross, Lords, and Attendants.

MACBETH: Here's our chief guest.
LADY MACBETH: If he had been forgotten,
It had been as a gap in our great feast,
And all-thing unbecoming.
MACBETH: To-night we hold a solemn supper sir,
And I'll request your presence.
BANQUO: Let your Highness
Command upon me, to the which my duties
Are with a most indissoluble tie
For ever knit.
MACBETH: Ride you this afternoon?
BANQUO: Ay, my good Lord.
MACBETH: We should have else desir'd your good advice
(Which still hath been both grave, and prosperous)
In this day's Council: but we'll take to-morrow.
Is't far you ride?
BANQUO: As far, my Lord, as will fill up the time

'Twixt this, and supper. Go not my horse the better,
I must become a borrower of the night,
For a dark hour, or twain.

MACBETH: Fail not our feast.

BANQUO: My Lord, I will not.

MACBETH: We hear our bloody cousins are bestow'd
In England, and in Ireland, not confessing
Their cruel parricide, filling their hearers
With strange invention. But of that to-morrow,
When therewithal, we shall have cause of state,
Craving us jointly. Hie you to horse:
Adieu, till you return at night.
Goes Fleance with you?

BANQUO: Ay, my good Lord: our time does call upon 's.

MACBETH: I wish your horses swift, and sure of foot:
And so I do commend you to their backs.
Farewell.

Exit Banquo.

Let every man be master of his time,
Till seven at night, to make society
The sweeter welcome:
We will keep ourself till supper-time alone:
While then, God be with you.

Exeunt all but Macbeth, and a servant.

Sirrah, a word with you: attend those men
Our pleasure?

SERVANT: They are, my Lord, without the Palace Gate.

MACBETH: Bring them before us.

Exit Servant.

To be thus, is nothing, but to be safely thus.
Our fears in Banquo stick deep,
And in his royalty of Nature reigns that
Which would be fear'd. 'Tis much he dares,

And to that dauntless temper of his mind,
He hath a wisdom, that doth guide his valour,
To act in safety. There is none but he,
Whose being I do fear: and under him,
My Genius is rebuk'd, as it is said
Mark Antony's was by Caesar. He chid the Sisters,
When first they put the name of King upon me,
And bad them speak to him. Then prophet-like,
They hail'd him father to a line of Kings.
Upon my head they plac'd a fruitless crown,
And put a barren sceptre in my gripe,
Thence to be wrench'd with an unlineal hand,
No son of mine succeeding: if't be so,
For Banquo's issue have I fil'd my mind,
For them, the gracious Duncan have I murther'd,
Put rancours in the vessel of my peace
Only for them, and mine eternal jewel
Given to the common Enemy of man,
To make them Kings, the seeds of Banquo Kings.
Rather than so, come Fate into the list,
And champion me to th' utterance.
Who's there?

       Enter Servant, and two Murtherers.
Now go to the door, and stay there till we call.
       Exit Servant.
Was it not yesterday we spoke together?
FIRST MURDERER: It was, so please your Highness.
MACBETH: Well then,
Now have you consider'd of my speeches:
Know, that it was he, in the times past,
Which held you so under fortune,
Which you thought had been our innocent self.
This I made good to you, in our last conference,

Pass'd in probation with you:
How you were borne in hand, how cross'd:
The instruments: who wrought with them:
And all things else, that might
To half a soul, and to a notion craz'd,
Say, Thus did Banquo.

FIRST MURDERER: You made it known to us.

MACBETH: I did so:
And went further, which is now
Our point of second meeting.
Do you find your patience so predominant,
In your nature, that you can let this go?
Are you so gospell'd, to pray for this good man,
And for his issue, whose heavy hand
Hath bow'd you to the grave, and beggar'd
Yours for ever?

FIRST MURDERER: We are men, my Liege.

MACBETH: Ay, in the catalogue ye go for men,
As hounds, and greyhounds, mongrels, spaniels, curs,
Shoughs, water-rugs, and demi-wolves are clept
All by the name of dogs: the valued file
Distinguishes the swift, the slow, the subtle,
The housekeeper, the hunter, every one
According to the gift, which bounteous Nature
Hath in him clos'd: whereby he does receive
Particular addition, from the bill,
That writes them all alike: and so of men.
Now, if you have a station in the file,
Not i' th' worst rank of manhood, say't,
And I will put that business in your bosoms,
Whose execution takes your enemy off,
Grapples you to the heart, and love of us,
Who wear our health but sickly in his life,

Which in his death were perfect.

SECOND MURDERER: I am one, my Liege,
Whom the vile blows and buffets of the world
Hath so incens'd, that I am reckless what I do,
To spite the world.

FIRST MURDERER: And I another,
So weary with disasters, tugg'd with Fortune,
That I would set my life on any chance,
To mend it, or be rid on't.

MACBETH: Both of you know Banquo was your enemy.

BOTH MURDERERS: True, my Lord.

MACBETH: So is he mine: and in such bloody distance,
That every minute of his being, thrusts
Against my near'st of life: and though I could
With barefac'd power sweep him from my sight,
And bid my will avouch it; yet I must not,
For certain friends that are both his, and mine,
Whose loves I may not drop, but wail his fall,
Who I myself struck down: and thence it is,
That I to your assistance do make love,
Masking the business from the common eye,
For sundry weighty reasons.

SECOND MURDERER: We shall, my Lord,
Perform what you command us.

FIRST MURDERER: Though our lives –

MACBETH: Your spirits shine through you.
Within this hour, at most,
I will advise you where to plant yourselves,
Acquaint you with the perfect spy o' th' time,
The moment on't, for't must be done to-night,
And something from the Palace: always thought,
That I require a clearness; and with him,
To leave no rubs nor botches in the work,

Fleance, his son, that keeps him company,
Whose absence is no less material to me,
Than is his father's, must embrace the fate
Of that dark hour: resolve yourselves apart,
I'll come to you anon.

BOTH MURDERERS: We are resolv'd, my Lord.

MACBETH: I'll call upon you straight: abide within,
It is concluded: Banquo, thy soul's flight,
If it find Heaven, must find it out to-night.

Exeunt.

III. 2

Enter Lady Macbeth, and a Servant.

LADY MACBETH: Is Banquo gone from Court?

SERVANT: Ay, Madam, but returns again to-night.

LADY MACBETH: Say to the King, I would attend his
leisure,
For a few words.

SERVANT: Madam, I will.

Exit.

LADY MACBETH: Nought's had, all's spent,
Where our desire is got without content:
'Tis safer, to be that which we destroy,
Than by destruction dwell in doubtful joy.

Enter Macbeth.

How now, my Lord, why do you keep alone?
Of sorriest fancies your companions making,
Using those thoughts, which should indeed have died
With them they think on: things without all remedy
Should be without regard: what's done, is done.

MACBETH: We have scorch'd the snake, not kill'd it:

    She'll close, and be herself, whilst our poor malice
Remains in danger of her former tooth.
But let the frame of things disjoint,
Both the worlds suffer,
Ere we will eat our meal in fear, and sleep
In the affliction of these terrible dreams,
That shake us nightly: better be with the dead,
Whom we, to gain our peace, have sent to peace,
Than on the torture of the mind to lie
In restless ecstasy.
Duncan is in his grave;
After life's fitful fever, he sleeps well,
Treason has done his worst: nor steel, nor poison,
Malice domestic, foreign levy, nothing,
Can touch him further.

LADY MACBETH: Come on:
    Gentle my Lord, sleek o'er your rugged looks,
Be bright and jovial among your guests to-night.

MACBETH: So shall I Love, and so I pray be you:
    Let your remembrance apply to Banquo,
Present him eminence, both with eye and tongue:
Unsafe the while, that we must lave
Our honours in these flattering streams,
And make our faces vizards to our hearts,
Disguising what they are.

LADY MACBETH: You must leave this.

MACBETH: O, full of scorpions is my mind, dear wife:
    Thou know'st, that Banquo and his Fleance lives.

LADY MACBETH: But in them, Nature's copy's not eterne.

MACBETH: There's comfort yet, they are assailable,
    Then be thou jocund: ere the bat hath flown
His cloister'd flight, ere to black Hecat's summons
The shard-borne beetle, with his drowsy hums,

Hath rung night's yawning peal,
There shall be done a deed of dreadful note.
LADY MACBETH: What's to be done?
MACBETH: Be innocent of the knowledge, dearest chuck,
Till thou applaud the deed: come, seeling Night,
Scarf up the tender eye of pitiful Day,
And with thy bloody and invisible hand
Cancel and tear to pieces that great bond,
Which keeps me pale. Light thickens,
And the crow makes wing to th' rooky wood:
Good things of Day begin to droop, and drowse,
Whiles Night's black agents to their preys do rouse.
Thou marvell'st at my words: but hold thee still,
Things bad begun, make strong themselves by ill:
So prithee go with me.

Exeunt.

III. 3

Enter three Murtherers.

FIRST MURDERER: But who did bid thee join with us?
THIRD MURDERER: Macbeth.
SECOND MURDERER: He needs not our mistrust, since he
delivers
Our offices, and what we have to do,
To the direction just.
FIRST MURDERER: Then stand with us:
The West yet glimmers with some streaks of day.
Now spurs the lated traveller apace,
To gain the timely inn, and near approaches
The subject of our watch.
THIRD MURDERER: Hark, I hear horses.

BANQUO (*within*): Give us a light there, hoa.
SECOND MURDERER: Then 'tis he:
  The rest, that are within the note of expectation,
  Already are i' th' Court.
FIRST MURDERER: His horses go about.
THIRD MURDERER: Almost a mile: but he does usually,
  So all men do, from hence to th' Palace Gate
  Make it their walk.

> *Enter Banquo, and Fleance, with a torch.*

SECOND MURDERER: A light, a light.
THIRD MURDERER: 'Tis he.
FIRST MURDERER: Stand to't.
BANQUO: It will be rain to-night.
FIRST MURDERER: Let it come down.
BANQUO: O, treachery!
  Fly good Fleance, fly, fly, fly.
  Thou mayst revenge. O slave!
THIRD MURDERER: Who did strike out the light?
FIRST MURDERER: Was't not the way?
THIRD MURDERER: There's but one down: the son is fled.
SECOND MURDERER: We have lost
  Best half of our affair.
FIRST MURDERER: Well, let's away, and say how much is
  done.

> *Exeunt.*

III. 4

> *Banquet prepared. Enter Macbeth, Lady Macbeth, Ross,
> Lennox, Lords, and Attendants.*

MACBETH: You know your own degrees, sit down:
  At first and last, the hearty welcome.

LORDS: Thanks to your Majesty.

MACBETH: Ourself will mingle with society,
And play the humble host:
Our hostess keeps her state, but in best time
We will require her welcome.

LADY MACBETH: Pronounce it for me sir, to all our friends,
For my heart speaks, they are welcome.

Enter First Murtherer.

MACBETH: See they encounter thee with their hearts' thanks,
Both sides are even: here I'll sit i' th' midst,
Be large in mirth, anon we'll drink a measure
The table round. There's blood upon thy face.

MURDERER: 'Tis Banquo's then.

MACBETH: 'Tis better thee without, than he within.
Is he dispatch'd?

MURDERER: My Lord his throat is cut, that I did for him.

MACBETH: Thou art the best o' th' cut-throats,
Yet he's good that did the like for Fleance.
If thou didst it, thou art the nonpareil.

MURDERER: Most Royal Sir,
Fleance is 'scap'd.

MACBETH: Then comes my fit again:
I had else been perfect;
Whole as the marble, founded as the rock,
As broad, and general, as the casing air:
But now I am cabin'd, cribb'd, confin'd, bound in
To saucy doubts, and fears. But Banquo's safe?

MURDERER: Ay, my good Lord: safe in a ditch he bides,
With twenty trenched gashes on his head;
The least a death to Nature.

MACBETH: Thanks for that:

There the grown serpent lies, the worm that's fled
Hath nature that in time will venom breed,
No teeth for th' present. Get thee gone, to-morrow
We'll hear ourselves again.

Exit Murderer.

LADY MACBETH: My Royal Lord,
You do not give the cheer: the feast is sold
That is not often vouch'd, while 'tis a-making:
'Tis given, with welcome: to feed were best at home:
From thence, the sauce to meat is ceremony,
Meeting were bare without it.

Enter the Ghost of Banquo, and sits in Macbeth's place.

MACBETH: Sweet remembrancer:
Now good digestion wait on appetite,
And health on both.

LENNOX: May't please your Highness sit.

MACBETH: Here had we now our country's honour, roof'd,
Were the grac'd person of our Banquo present:
Who, may I rather challenge for unkindness,
Than pity for mischance.

ROSS: His absence, Sir,
Lays blame upon his promise. Please't your Highness
To grace us with your royal company?

MACBETH: The table's full.

LENNOX: Here is a place reserv'd Sir.

MACBETH: Where?

LENNOX: Here my good Lord.
What is't that moves your Highness?

MACBETH: Which of you have done this?

LORDS: What, my good Lord?

MACBETH: Thou canst not say I did it: never shake
Thy gory locks at me.

ROSS: Gentlemen rise, his Highness is not well.

LADY MACBETH: Sit worthy friends: my Lord is often thus,
And hath been from his youth. Pray you keep seat,
The fit is momentary, upon a thought
He will again be well. If much you note him,
You shall offend him, and extend his passion,
Feed, and regard him not. Are you a man?

MACBETH: Ay, and a bold one, that dare look on that
Which might appal the Devil.

LADY MACBETH: O proper stuff:
This is the very painting of your fear:
This is the air-drawn dagger which you said
Led you to Duncan. O, these flaws and starts
(Impostors to true fear) would well become
A woman's story, at a winter's fire
Authoriz'd by her grandam: shame itself,
Why do you make such faces? When all's done
You look but on a stool.

MACBETH: Prithee see there:
Behold, look, lo, how say you?
Why what care I, if thou canst nod, speak too.
If charnel-houses, and our graves must send
Those that we bury, back; our monuments
Shall be the maws of kites.

Exit Ghost.

LADY MACBETH: What? quite unmann'd in folly.

MACBETH: If I stand here, I saw him.

LADY MACBETH: Fie for shame.

MACBETH: Blood hath been shed ere now, i' th' olden time
Ere humane statute purg'd the gentle weal:
Ay, and since too, murthers have been perform'd
Too terrible for the ear. The time has been,
That when the brains were out, the man would die,

And there an end: but now they rise again
With twenty mortal murthers on their crowns,
And push us from our stools. This is more strange
Than such a murther is.

LADY MACBETH: My worthy Lord
Your noble friends do lack you.

MACBETH: I do forget:
Do not muse at me my most worthy friends,
I have a strange infirmity, which is nothing
To those that know me. Come, love and health to all,
Then I'll sit down: give me some wine, fill full.

Enter Ghost.

I drink to th' general joy o' th' whole table,
And to our dear friend Banquo, whom we miss:
Would he were here: to all, and him we thirst,
And all to all.

LORDS: Our duties, and the pledge.

MACBETH: Avaunt, and quit my sight, let the earth hide
thee:
Thy bones are marrowless, thy blood is cold:
Thou hast no speculation in those eyes
Which thou dost glare with.

LADY MACBETH: Think of this good Peers
But as a thing of custom: 'tis no other,
Only it spoils the pleasure of the time.

MACBETH: What man dare, I dare:
Approach thou like the rugged Russian bear,
The arm'd rhinoceros, or th' Hyrcan tiger,
Take any shape but that, and my firm nerves
Shall never tremble. Or be alive again,
And dare me to the desert with thy sword:
If trembling I inhabit then, protest me
The baby of a girl. Hence horrible shadow,

Unreal mockery hence.

Exit Ghost.

Why so, being gone

I am a man again: pray you sit still.

LADY MACBETH: You have displac'd the mirth,
Broke the good meeting, with most admir'd disorder.

MACBETH: Can such things be,
And overcome us like a summer's cloud,
Without our special wonder? You make me strange
Even to the disposition that I owe,
When now I think you can behold such sights,
And keep the natural ruby of your cheeks,
When mine is blanch'd with fear.

ROSS: What sights my Lord?

LADY MACBETH: I pray you speak not: he grows worse
and worse:
Question enrages him: at once, good night.
Stand not upon the order of your going,
But go at once.

LENNOX: Good night, and better health
Attend his Majesty.

LADY MACBETH: A kind good night to all.

Exit Lords.

MACBETH: It will have blood they say:
Blood will have blood:
Stones have been known to move, and trees to speak:
Augurs, and understood relations, have
By magot-pies, and choughs, and rooks brought forth
The secret'st man of blood. What is the night?

LADY MACBETH: Almost at odds with morning, which is
which.

MACBETH: How say'st thou that Macduff denies his person
At our great bidding?

LADY MACBETH : Did you send to him Sir?
MACBETH: I hear it by the way: but I will send:
There's not a one of them but in his house
I keep a servant fee'd. I will to-morrow
(And betimes I will) to the Weird Sisters.
More shall they speak: for now I am bent to know
By the worst means, the worst; for mine own good,
All causes shall give way. I am in blood
Stepp'd in so far, that should I wade no more,
Returning were as tedious as go o'er:
Strange things I have in head, that will to hand,
Which must be acted, ere they may be scann'd.
LADY MACBETH: You lack the season of all natures, sleep.
MACBETH: Come, we'll to sleep. my strange and self-
    abuse
Is the initiate fear, that wants hard use:
We are yet but young in deed.

                    Exeunt.

III. 5

Thunder. Enter the three Witches, meeting Hecat.
FIRST WITCH: Why how now Hecat, you look angerly?
HECAT: Have I not reason, beldams as you are?
Saucy, and overbold, how did you dare
To trade, and traffic with Macbeth,
In riddles, and affairs of death;
And I the mistress of your charms,
The close contriver of all harms,
Was never call'd to bear my part,
Or show the glory of our art?
And which is worse, all you have done

Hath been but for a wayward son,
Spiteful, and wrathful, who (as others do)
Loves for his own ends, not for you.
But make amends now: get you gone,
And at the pit of Acheron
Meet me i' th' morning: thither he
Will come, to know his destiny.
Your vessels, and your spells provide,
Your charms, and every thing beside;
I am for th' air: this night I'll spend
Unto a dismal, and a fatal end.
Great business must be wrought ere noon.
Upon the corner of the moon
There hangs a vaporous drop, profound,
I'll catch it ere it come to ground;
And that distill'd by magic sleights,
Shall raise such artificial sprites,
As by the strength of their illusion,
Shall draw him on to his confusion.
He shall spurn Fate, scorn Death, and bear
His hopes 'bove wisdom, grace, and fear:
And you all know, security
Is mortals' chiefest enemy.

Music, and a song.

Hark, I am call'd: my little spirit see,
Sits in a foggy cloud, and stays for me.

Song within 'Come away, come away,' etc.

FIRST WITCH: Come, let's make haste, she'll soon be
    Back again.

Exeunt.

III. 6

Enter Lennox, and another Lord.

LENNOX: My former speeches,
  Have but hit your thoughts
  Which can interpret farther: only I say
  Things have been strangely borne. The gracious Duncan
  Was pitied of Macbeth: marry he was dead:
  And the right valiant Banquo walk'd too late,
  Whom you may say (if't please you) Fleance kill'd,
  For Fleance fled: men must not walk too late.
  Who cannot want the thought, how monstrous
  It was for Malcolm, and for Donalbain
  To kill their gracious father? Damned fact,
  How it did grieve Macbeth! Did he not straight
  In pious rage, the two delinquents tear,
  That were the slaves of drink, and thralls of sleep?
  Was not that nobly done? Ay, and wisely too:
  For 'twould have anger'd any heart alive
  To hear the men deny't. So that I say,
  He has borne all things well, and I do think,
  That had he Duncan's sons under his key,
  (As, and't please Heaven he shall not) they should find
  What 'twere to kill a father: so should Fleance.
  But peace; for from broad words, and 'cause he fail'd
  His presence at the tyrant's feast, I hear
  Macduff lives in disgrace. Sir, can you tell
  Where he bestows himself?
LORD: The son of Duncan
  (From whom this tyrant holds the due of birth)
  Lives in the English Court, and is receiv'd
  Of the most pious Edward, with such grace,

That the malevolence of Fortune nothing
Takes from his high respect. Thither Macduff
Is gone, to pray the holy King, upon his aid
To wake Northumberland, and warlike Siward,
That by the help of these (with Him above
To ratify the work) we may again
Give to our tables meat, sleep to our nights:
Free from our feasts, and banquets bloody knives;
Do faithful homage, and receive free honours,
All which we pine for now. And this report
Hath so exasperate the King, that he
Prepares for some attempt of war.

LENNOX: Sent he to Macduff?

LORD: He did: and with an absolute Sir, not I
The cloudy messenger turns me his back,
And hums; as who should say, you'll rue the time
That clogs me with this answer.

LENNOX: And that well might
Advise him to a caution, to hold what distance
His wisdom can provide. Some holy Angel
Fly to the Court of England, and unfold
His message ere he come, that a swift blessing
May soon return to this our suffering country,
Under a hand accurs'd.

LORD: I'll send my prayers with him.

Exeunt.

IV.1

Thunder. Enter the three Witches.

FIRST WITCH: Thrice the brinded cat hath mew'd.

SECOND WITCH: Thrice, and once the hedge-pig whin'd

THIRD WITCH: Harpier cries, 'tis time, 'tis time.
FIRST WITCH: Round about the cauldron go:
    In the poison'd entrails throw.
    Toad, that under cold stone,
    Days and nights, has thirty one:
    Swelter'd venom sleeping got,
    Boil thou first i' th' charmed pot.
ALL: Double, double, toil and trouble;
    Fire burn, and cauldron bubble.
SECOND WITCH: Fillet of a fenny snake,
    In the cauldron boil and bake:
    Eye of newt, and toe of frog,
    Wool of bat, and tongue of dog:
    Adder's fork, and blind-worm's sting,
    Lizard's leg, and howlet's wing:
    For a charm of powerful trouble,
    Like a hell-broth, boil and bubble.
ALL: Double, double, toil and trouble,
    Fire burn, and cauldron bubble.
THIRD WITCH: Scale of dragon, tooth of wolf,
    Witch's mummy, maw, and gulf
    Of the ravin'd salt-sea shark:
    Root of hemlock, digg'd i' th' dark:
    Liver of blaspheming Jew,
    Gall of goat, and slips of yew,
    Sliver'd in the moon's eclipse:
    Nose of Turk, and Tartar's lips:
    Finger of birth-strangled babe,
    Ditch-deliver'd by a drab,
    Make the gruel thick, and slab.
    Add thereto a tiger's chaudron,
    For th' ingredients of our cauldron.
ALL: Double, double, toil and trouble,

Fire burn, and cauldron bubble.

SECOND WITCH: Cool it with a baboon's blood,
Then the charm is firm and good.

Enter Hecat, to the other three Witches.

HECAT: O well done: I commend your pains,
And every one shall share i' th' gains:
And now about the cauldron sing
Like elves and fairies in a ring,
Enchanting all that you put in.

Music and a song: 'Black spirits,' etc.

SECOND WITCH: By the pricking of my thumbs,
Something wicked this way comes:
Open locks, whoever knocks.

Enter Macbeth.

MACBETH: How now you secret, black, and midnight
hags?
What is't you do?

ALL: A deed without a name.

MACBETH: I conjure you, by that which you profess,
(Howe'er you come to know it) answer me:
Though you untie the winds, and let them fight
Against the churches: though the yesty waves
Confound and swallow navigation up:
Though bladed corn be lodg'd, and trees blown down,
Though castles topple on their warders' heads:
Though palaces, and pyramids do slope
Their heads to their foundations: though the treasure
Of Nature's germen, tumble all together,
Even till destruction sicken: answer me
To what I ask you.

FIRST WITCH: Speak.

SECOND WITCH: Demand.

THIRD WITCH: We'll answer.

FIRST WITCH: Say, if thou'dst rather hear it from our
    mouths,
Or from our masters.
MACBETH: Call 'em: let me see 'em.
FIRST WITCH: Pour in sow's blood, that hath eaten
    Her nine farrow: grease that's sweaten
    From the murderer's gibbet, throw
    Into the flame.
ALL: Come high or low:
    Thyself and office deftly show.
       Thunder. First Apparition, an Armed Head.
MACBETH: Tell me, thou unknown power.
FIRST WITCH: He knows thy thought:
    Hear his speech, but say thou nought.
FIRST APPARITION: Macbeth, Macbeth, Macbeth:
    Beware Macduff,
    Beware the Thane of Fife: dismiss me. Enough.
       He descends.
MACBETH: Whate'er thou art, for thy good caution,
    thanks,
Thou hast harp'd my fear aright. But one word more.
FIRST WITCH: He will not be commanded: here's another,
More potent than the first.
       Thunder. Second Apparition, a Bloody Child.
SECOND APPARITION: Macbeth, Macbeth, Macbeth.
MACBETH: Had I three ears, I'ld hear thee.
SECOND APPARITION: Be bloody, bold, and resolute:
    Laugh to scorn
The power of man: for none of woman born
Shall harm Macbeth.
       Descends.
MACBETH: Then live Macduff: what need I fear of thee?
But yet I'll make assurance double sure,

And take a bond of Fate: thou shalt not live,
That I may tell pale-hearted Fear, it lies;
And sleep in spite of thunder.
           Thunder. Third Apparition: a Child crowned,
                with a tree in his hand.
What is this, that rises like the issue of a King,
And wears upon his baby-brow, the round
And top of sovereignty?
ALL: Listen, but speak not to't.
THIRD APPARITION: Be lion-mettled, proud, and take no
    care:
Who chafes, who frets, or where conspirers are:
Macbeth shall never vanquish'd be, until
Great Birnam Wood, to high Dunsinane Hill
Shall come against him.
                          Descends.
MACBETH: That will never be:
Who can impress the forest, bid the tree
Unfix his earth-bound root? Sweet bodements, good:
Rebellion's head, rise never till the Wood
Of Birnam rise, and our high-plac'd Macbeth
Shall live the lease of Nature, pay his breath
To time, and mortal custom. Yet my heart
Throbs to know one thing: tell me, if your Art
Can tell so much: shall Banquo's issue ever
Reign in this Kingdom?
ALL: Seek to know no more.
MACBETH: I will be satisfied. Deny me this,
And an eternal curse fall on you: let me know.
Why sinks that cauldron? and what noise is this?
                          Oboes.
FIRST WITCH: Show.
SECOND WITCH: Show.

THIRD WITCH: Show.

ALL: Show his eyes, and grieve his heart,
Come like shadows, so depart.

A show of eight Kings, and Banquo last, with a glass in his hand.

MACBETH: Thou art too like the spirit of Banquo: down:
Thy crown does sear mine eye-balls. And thy hair,
Thou other gold-bound brow, is like the first:
A third is like the former. Filthy hags,
Why do you show me this? – A fourth? Start eyes!
What will the line stretch out to th' crack of Doom?
Another yet? A seventh? I'll see no more:
And yet the eighth appears, who bears a glass,
Which shows me many more; and some I see,
That two-fold balls, and treble sceptres carry.
Horrible sight: now I see 'tis true,
For the blood-bolter'd Banquo smiles upon me,
And points at them for his. What? is this so?

FIRST WITCH: Ay Sir, all this is so. But why
Stands Macbeth thus amazedly?
Come sisters, cheer we up his sprites,
And show the best of our delights.
I'll charm the air to give a sound,
While you perform your antic round:
That this great King may kindly say,
Our duties did his welcome pay.

    Music. The Witches dance, and vanish.

MACBETH: Where are they? Gone?
Let this pernicious hour,
Stand aye accursed in the Calendar.
Come in, without there.

      Enter Lennox.

LENNOX: What's your Grace's will?

MACBETH: Saw you the Weird Sisters?

LENNOX: No my Lord.

MACBETH: Came they not by you?

LENNOX: No indeed my Lord.

MACBETH: Infected be the air whereon they ride,
And damn'd all those that trust them. I did hear
The galloping of horse. Who was't came by?

LENNOX: 'Tis two or three my Lord, that bring you
word:
Macduff is fled to England.

MACBETH: Fled to England?

LENNOX: Ay, my good Lord.

MACBETH: Time, thou anticipat'st my dread exploits:
The flighty purpose never is o'ertook
Unless the deed go with it. From this moment,
The very firstlings of my heart shall be
The firstlings of my hand. And even now
To crown my thoughts with acts, be it thought and
done:
The Castle of Macduff, I will surprise,
Seize upon Fife: give to th' edge o' th' sword
His wife, his babes, and all unfortunate souls
That trace him in his line. No boasting like a fool,
This deed I'll do, before this purpose cool,
But no more sights. Where are these gentlemen?
Come bring me where they are.

Exeunt.

Enter Macduff's wife, her Son, and Ross.

LADY MACDUFF: What had he done, to make him fly the
 land?

ROSS: You must have patience Madam.

LADY MACDUFF: He had none:
 His flight was madness: when our actions do not,
 Our fears do make us traitors.

ROSS: You know not
 Whether it was his wisdom, or his fear.

LADY MACDUFF: Wisdom? to leave his wife, to leave his
 babes,
 His mansion, and his titles, in a place
 From whence himself does fly? He loves us not,
 He wants the natural touch. For the poor wren,
 (The most diminutive of birds) will fight,
 Her young ones in her nest, against the owl:
 All is the fear, and nothing is the love;
 As little is the wisdom, where the flight
 So runs against all reason.

ROSS: My dearest coz,
 I pray you school yourself. But for your husband,
 He is noble, wise, judicious, and best knows
 The fits o' th' season. I dare not speak much further,
 But cruel are the times, when we are traitors
 And do not know ourselves: when we hold rumour
 From what we fear, yet know not what we fear,
 But float upon a wild and violent sea
 Each way, and move. I take my leave of you:
 Shall not be long but I'll be here again:
 Things at the worst will cease, or else climb upward,

To what they were before. My pretty cousin,
Blessing upon you.

LADY MACDUFF: Father'd he is,
And yet he's fatherless.

ROSS: I am so much a fool, should I stay longer
It would be my disgrace, and your discomfort.
I take my leave at once.

Exit Ross.

LADY MACDUFF: Sirrah, your father's dead,
And what will you do now?   How will you live?

SON: As birds do, Mother.

LADY MACDUFF: What with worms, and flies?

SON: With what I get I mean, and so do they.

LADY MACDUFF: Poor bird,
Thou'ldst never fear the net, nor lime,
The pitfall, nor the gin.

SON: Why should I, mother?
Poor birds they are not set for:
My father is not dead for all your saying.

LADY MACDUFF: Yes, he is dead:
How wilt thou do for a father?

SON: Nay how will you do for a husband?

LADY MACDUFF: Why I can buy me twenty at any market.

SON: Then you'll buy 'em to sell again.

LADY MACDUFF: Thou speak'st with all thy wit,
And yet i' faith with wit enough for thee.

SON: Was my father a traitor, Mother?

LADY MACDUFF: Ay, that he was.

SON: What is a traitor?

LADY MACDUFF: Why one that swears, and lies.

SON: And be all traitors, that do so?

LADY MACDUFF: Every one that does so, is a traitor, and
must be hang'd.

SON: And must they all be hang'd, that swear and lie?

LADY MACDUFF: Every one.

SON: Who must hang them?

LADY MACDUFF: Why, the honest men.

SON: Then the liars and swearers are fools: for there
are liars and swearers enow, to beat the honest men,
and hang up them.

LADY MACDUFF: Now God help thee, poor monkey:
But how wilt thou do for a father?

SON: If he were dead, you'ld weep for him: if you would
not, it were a good sign, that I should quickly have a
new father.

LADY MACDUFF: Poor prattler, how thou talk'st!

Enter a Messenger.

MESSENGER: Bless you fair Dame: I am not to you known,
Though in your state of honour I am perfect;
I doubt some danger does approach you nearly.
If you will take a homely man's advice,
Be not found here: hence with your little ones.
To fright you thus, methinks I am too savage:
To do worse to you, were fell cruelty,
Which is too nigh your person. Heaven preserve you,
I dare abide no longer.

Exit Messenger.

LADY MACDUFF: Whither should I fly?
I have done no harm. But I remember now
I am in this earthly world: where to do harm
Is often laudable, to do good sometime
Accounted dangerous folly. Why then, alas,
Do I put up that womanly defence,
To say I have done no harm?
What are these faces?

Enter Murtherers.

FIRST MURDERER: Where is your husband?
LADY MACDUFF: I hope in no place so unsanctified,
  Where such as thou mayst find him.
FIRST MURDERER: He's a traitor.
SON: Thou liest thou shag-ear'd villain.
FIRST MURDERER: What you egg?
  Young fry of treachery!
SON: He has kill'd me Mother,
  Run away I pray you!

Exit crying Murther.

IV.3

Enter Malcolm and Macduff.

MALCOLM: Let us seek out some desolate shade, and there
  Weep our sad bosoms empty.
MACDUFF: Let us rather
  Hold fast the mortal sword: and like good men,
  Bestride our down-fall'n birthdom: each new morn,
  New widows howl, new orphans cry, new sorrows
  Strike heaven on the face, that it resounds
  As if it felt with Scotland, and yell'd out
  Like syllable of dolour.
MALCOLM: What I believe, I'll wail;
  What know, believe; and what I can redress,
  As I shall find the time to friend: I will.
  What you have spoke, it may be so perchance.
  This Tyrant, whose sole name blisters our tongues,
  Was once thought honest: you have lov'd him well,
  He hath not touch'd you yet. I am young, but something
  You may discern of him through me, and wisdom

To offer up a weak, poor innocent lamb
T' appease an angry god.
MACDUFF: I am not treacherous.
MALCOLM: But Macbeth is.
A good and virtuous nature may recoil
In an imperial charge. But I shall crave your pardon:
That which you are, my thoughts cannot transpose;
Angels are bright still, though the brightest fell.
Though all things foul, would wear the brows of grace
Yet Grace must still look so.
MACDUFF: I have lost my hopes.
MALCOLM: Perchance even there
Where I did find my doubts.
Why in that rawness left you wife, and child?
Those precious motives, those strong knots of love,
Without leave-taking? I pray you,
Let not my jealousies, be your dishonours,
But mine own safeties: you may be rightly just,
Whatever I shall think.
MACDUFF: Bleed, bleed poor Country.
Great Tyranny, lay thou thy basis sure,
For goodness dare not check thee: wear thou thy wrongs,
The title is affeer'd. Fare thee well Lord,
I would not be the villain that thou think'st,
For the whole space that's in the Tyrant's grasp,
And the rich East to boot.
MALCOLM: Be not offended:
I speak not as in absolute fear of you:
I think our country sinks beneath the yoke,
It weeps, it bleeds, and each new day a gash
Is added to her wounds. I think withal,
There would be hands uplifted in my right:
And here from gracious England have I offer

Of goodly thousands. But for all this,
When I shall tread upon the Tyrant's head,
Or wear it on my sword; yet my poor Country
Shall have more vices than it had before,
More suffer, and more sundry ways than ever,
By him that shall succeed.

MACDUFF: What should he be?

MALCOLM: It is myself I mean: in whom I know
All the particulars of vice so grafted,
That when they shall be open'd, black Macbeth
Will seem as pure as snow, and the poor State
Esteem him as a lamb, being compar'd
With my confineless harms.

MACDUFF: Not in the legions
Of horrid Hell, can come a devil more damn'd
In evils, to top Macbeth.

MALCOLM: I grant him bloody,
Luxurious, avaricious, false, deceitful,
Sudden, malicious, smacking of every sin
That has a name. But there's no bottom, none
In my voluptuousness: your wives, your daughters,
Your matrons, and your maids, could not fill up
The cistern of my lust, and my desire
All continent impediments would o'erbear
That did oppose my will. Better Macbeth,
Than such an one to reign.

MACDUFF: Boundless intemperance
In Nature is a tyranny: it hath been
Th' untimely emptying of the happy throne,
And fall of many Kings. But fear not yet
To take upon you what is yours: you may
Convey your pleasures in a spacious plenty,
And yet seem cold. The time you may so hoodwink:

We have willing dames enough: there cannot be
That vulture in you, to devour so many
As will to greatness dedicate themselves,
Finding it so inclin'd.
MALCOLM: With this, there grows
In my most ill-compos'd affection, such
A stanchless avarice, that were I King,
I should cut off the Nobles for their lands,
Desire his jewels, and this other's house,
And my more-having, would be as a sauce
To make me hunger more, that I should forge
Quarrels unjust against the good and loyal,
Destroying them for wealth.
MACDUFF: This avarice
Sticks deeper: grows with more pernicious root
Than summer-seeming lust: and it hath been
The sword of our slain Kings: yet do not fear,
Scotland hath foisons, to fill up your will
Of your mere own. All these are portable,
With other graces weigh'd.
MALCOLM: But I have none. The king-becoming graces,
As justice, verity, temperance, stableness,
Bounty, perseverance, mercy, lowliness,
Devotion, patience, courage, fortitude,
I have no relish of them, but abound
In the division of each several crime,
Acting it many ways. Nay, had I power, I should
Pour the sweet milk of concord, into Hell,
Uproar the universal peace, confound
All unity on earth.
MACDUFF: O Scotland, Scotland.
MALCOLM: If such a one be fit to govern, speak:
I am as I have spoken.

MACDUFF: Fit to govern? No not to live. O Nation
   miserable!
  With an untitled Tyrant, bloody scepter'd,
  When shalt thou see thy wholesome days again?
  Since that the truest issue of thy Throne
  By his own interdiction stands accus'd,
  And does blaspheme his breed? Thy Royal Father
  Was a most sainted King: the Queen that bore thee,
  Oftener upon her knees, than on her feet,
  Died every day she liv'd. Fare thee well,
  These evils thou repeat'st upon thyself,
  Have banish'd me from Scotland. O my breast,
  Thy hope ends here.
MALCOLM: Macduff, this noble passion,
  Child of integrity, hath from my soul
  Wip'd the black scruples, reconcil'd my thoughts
  To thy good truth, and honour. Devilish Macbeth,
  By many of these trains, hath sought to win me
  Into his power: and modest wisdom plucks me
  From over-credulous haste: but God above
  Deal between thee and me; for even now
  I put myself to thy direction, and
  Unspeak mine own detraction. Here abjure
  The taints, and blames I laid upon myself,
  For strangers to my nature. I am yet
  Unknown to woman, never was forsworn,
  Scarcely have coveted what was mine own,
  At no time broke my faith, would not betray
  The Devil to his fellow, and delight
  No less in truth than life. My first false speaking
  Was this upon myself. What I am truly
  Is thine, and my poor Country's to command:
  Whither indeed, before thy here approach

Old Siward with ten thousand warlike men
Already at a point, was setting forth:
Now we'll together, and the chance of goodness
Be like our warranted quarrel. Why are you silent?

MACDUFF: Such welcome, and unwelcome things at once
'Tis hard to reconcile.

Enter a Doctor.

MALCOLM: Well, more anon. Comes the King forth
I pray you?

DOCTOR: Ay Sir: there are a crew of wretched souls
That stay his cure: their malady convinces
The great assay of Art. But at his touch,
Such sanctity hath Heaven given his hand,
They presently amend.

MALCOLM: I thank you doctor.

Exit.

MACDUFF: What's the disease he means?

MALCOLM: 'Tis call'd the Evil.
A most miraculous work in this good King,
Which often since my here remain in England,
I have seen him do: how he solicits Heaven
Himself best knows: but strangely-visited people,
All swoln and ulcerous, pitiful to the eye,
The mere despair of surgery, he cures,
Hanging a golden stamp about their necks,
Put on with holy prayers, and 'tis spoken,
To the succeeding royalty he leaves
The healing benediction. With this strange virtue,
He hath a heavenly gift of prophecy,
And sundry blessings hang about his Throne,
That speak him full of grace.

Enter Ross.

MACDUFF: See who comes here.

MALCOLM: My countryman: but yet I know him not.

MACDUFF: My ever gentle cousin, welcome hither.

MALCOLM: I know him now. Good God betimes remove
The means that makes us strangers.

ROSS: Sir, amen.

MACDUFF: Stands Scotland where it did?

ROSS: Alas poor country,
Almost afraid to know itself. It cannot
Be call'd our mother, but our grave; where nothing
But who knows nothing, is once seen to smile:
Where sighs, and groans, and shrieks that rent the air
Are made, not mark'd: where violent sorrow seems
A modern ecstasy: the dead man's knell,
Is there scarce ask'd for who, and good men's lives
Expire before the flowers in their caps,
Dying, or ere they sicken.

MACDUFF: O relation too nice, and yet too true.

MALCOLM: What's the newest grief?

ROSS: That of an hour's age, doth hiss the speaker,
Each minute teems a new one.

MACDUFF: How does my wife?

ROSS: Why well.

MACDUFF: And all my children?

ROSS: Well too.

MACDUFF: The Tyrant has not batter'd at their peace?

ROSS: No, they were well at peace, when I did leave 'em.

MACDUFF: Be not a niggard of your speech: how goes 't?

ROSS: When I came hither to transport the tidings
Which I have heavily borne, there ran a rumour
Of many worthy fellows, that were out,
Which was to my belief witness'd the rather,
For that I saw the Tyrant's power a-foot.
Now is the time of help: your eye in Scotland

Would create soldiers, make our women fight,
To doff their dire distresses.
MALCOLM: Be 't their comfort
We are coming thither: gracious England hath
Lent us good Siward, and ten thousand men,
An older, and a better soldier, none
That Christendom gives out.
ROSS: Would I could answer
This comfort with the like. But I have words
That would be howl'd out in the desert air,
Where hearing should not latch them.
MACDUFF: What concern they,
The general cause, or is it a fee-grief
Due to some single breast?
ROSS: No mind that's honest
But in it shares some woe, though the main part
Pertains to you alone.
MACDUFF: If it be mine
Keep it not from me, quickly let me have it.
ROSS: Let not your ears despise my tongue for ever.
Which shall possess them with the heaviest sound
That ever yet they heard.
MACDUFF: Humh: I guess at it.
ROSS: Your Castle is surpris'd: your wife, and babes
Savagely slaughter'd: to relate the manner
Were on the quarry of these murther'd deer
To add the death of you.
MALCOLM: Merciful Heavens:
What man, ne'er pull your hat upon your brows:
Give sorrow words; the grief that does not speak,
Whispers the o'er-fraught heart, and bids it break.
MACDUFF: My children too?
ROSS: Wife, children, servants, all that could be found.

MACDUFF: And I must be from thence? My wife kill'd too?
ROSS: I have said.
MALCOLM: Be comforted.
   Let's make us medicines of our great revenge,
   To cure this deadly grief.
MACDUFF: He has no children. All my pretty ones?
   Did you say All? O hell-kite! All?
   What, All my pretty chickens, and their dam
   At one fell swoop?
MALCOLM: Dispute it like a man.
MACDUFF: I shall do so:
   But I must also feel it as a man;
   I cannot but remember such things were
   That were most precious to me: did Heaven look on,
   And would not take their part? Sinful Macduff,
   They were all struck for thee: naught that I am,
   Not for their own demerits, but for mine
   Fell slaughter on their souls: Heaven rest them now.
MALCOLM: Be this the whetstone of your sword, let grief
   Convert to anger: blunt not the heart, enrage it.
MACDUFF: O I could play the woman with mine eyes,
   And braggart with my tongue. But gentle Heavens,
   Cut short all intermission: front to front,
   Bring thou this fiend of Scotland, and myself;
   Within my sword's length set him, if he scape
   Heaven forgive him too.
MALCOLM: This tune goes manly:
   Come go we to the King, our power is ready,
   Our lack is nothing but our leave. Macbeth
   Is ripe for shaking, and the Powers above
   Put on their instruments: receive what cheer you may,
   The night is long, that never finds the day.
                              Exeunt.

Enter a Doctor of Physic, and a Waiting Gentlewoman.

DOCTOR: I have two nights watch'd with you, but can perceive no truth in your report. When was it she last walk'd?

GENTLEWOMAN: Since his Majesty went into the field, I have seen her rise from her bed, throw her nightgown upon her, unlock her closet, take forth paper, fold it, write upon 't, read it, afterwards seal it, and again return to bed; yet all this while in a most fast sleep.

DOCTOR: A great perturbation in nature, to receive at once the benefit of sleep, and do the effects of watching. In this slumbery agitation, besides her walking, and other actual performances, what (at any time) have you heard her say?

GENTLEWOMAN: That sir, which I will not report after her.

DOCTOR: You may to me, and 'tis most meet you should.

GENTLEWOMAN: Neither to you, nor any one, having no witness to confirm my speech.

Enter Lady Macbeth, with a taper.

Lo you, here she comes: this is her very guise, and upon my life fast asleep: observe her, stand close.

DOCTOR: How came she by that light?

GENTLEWOMAN: Why it stood by her: she has light by her continually, 'tis her command.

DOCTOR: You see her eyes are open.

GENTLEWOMAN: Ay but their sense are shut.

DOCTOR: What is it she does now?

Look how she rubs her hands.

GENTLEWOMAN: It is an accustom'd action with her, to

seem thus washing her hands: I have known her continue in this a quarter of an hour.

LADY MACBETH: Yet here's a spot.

DOCTOR: Hark, she speaks, I will set down what comes from her, to satisfy my remembrance the more strongly.

LADY MACBETH: Out damned spot: out I say. One: two: why then 'tis time to do 't: Hell is murky. Fie, my Lord, fie, a soldier, and afear'd? what need we fear? who knows it, when none can call our power to accompt: yet who would have thought the old man to have had so much blood in him.

DOCTOR: Do you mark that?

LADY MACBETH: The Thane of Fife, had a wife: where is she now? What will these hands ne'er be clean? No more o' that my Lord, no more o' that: you mar all with this starting.

DOCTOR: Go to, go to:
You have known what you should not.

GENTLEWOMAN: She has spoke what she should not, I am sure of that: Heaven knows what she has known.

LADY MACBETH: Here's the smell of the blood still: all the perfumes of Arabia will not sweeten this little hand. Oh, oh, oh.

DOCTOR: What a sigh is there! The heart is sorely charg'd.

GENTLEWOMAN: I would not have such a heart in my bosom, for the dignity of the whole body.

DOCTOR: Well, well, well.

GENTLEWOMAN: Pray God it be sir.

DOCTOR: This disease is beyond my practice: yet I have known those which have walk'd in their sleep, who have died holily in their beds.

LADY MACBETH: Wash your hands, put on your night-

gown, look not so pale: I tell you yet again Banquo's
buried; he cannot come out on 's grave.

DOCTOR: Even so?

LADY MACBETH: To bed, to bed: there's knocking at the
gate: come, come, come, come, give me your hand:
what's done, cannot be undone. To bed, to bed, to bed.
Exit Lady Macbeth.

DOCTOR: Will she go now to bed?

GENTLEWOMAN: Directly.

DOCTOR: Foul whisperings are abroad: unnatural deeds
Do breed unnatural troubles: infected minds
To their deaf pillows will discharge their secrets:
More needs she the divine, than the physician:
God, God forgive us all. Look after her,
Remove from her the means of all annoyance,
And still keep eyes upon her: so good night,
My mind she has mated, and amaz'd my sight.
I think, but dare not speak.

GENTLEWOMAN: Good night good doctor.

Exeunt.

V.2

Drum and colours. Enter Menteith, Caithness, Angus,
Lennox, Soldiers.

MENTIETH: The English power is near, led on by Malcolm,
His uncle Siward, and the good Macduff.
Revenges burn in them: for their dear causes
Would to the bleeding, and the grim alarm
Excite the mortified man.

ANGUS: Near Birnam wood
Shall we well meet them, that way are they coming.

CAITHNESS: Who knows if Donalbain be with his brother?
LENNOX: For certain sir, he is not: I have a file
    Of all the gentry; there is Siward's son,
    And many unrough youths, that even now
    Protest their first of manhood.
MENTIETH: What does the tyrant?
CAITHNESS: Great Dunsinane he strongly fortifies:
    Some say he's mad: others, that lesser hate him,
    Do call it valiant fury, but for certain
    He cannot buckle his distemper'd cause
    Within the belt of rule.
ANGUS: Now does he feel
    His secret murthers sticking on his hands,
    Now minutely revolts upbraid his faith-breach:
    Those he commands, move only in command,
    Nothing in love: now does he feel his title
    Hang loose about him, like a giant's robe
    Upon a dwarfish thief.
MENTIETH: Who then shall blame
    His pester'd senses to recoil, and start,
    When all that is within him, does condemn
    Itself, for being there?
CAITHNESS: Well, march we on,
    To give obedience, where 'tis truly ow'd:
    Meet we the medicine of the sickly weal,
    And with him pour we in our country's purge,
    Each drop of us.
LENNOX: Or so much as it needs,
    To dew the sovereign flower, and drown the weeds:
    Make we our march towards Birnam.

               Exeunt marching.

V. 3

Enter Macbeth, Doctor, and Attendants.

MACBETH: Bring me no more reports, let them fly all:
  Till Birnam wood remove to Dunsinane,
  I cannot taint with fear. What's the boy Malcolm?
  Was he not born of woman? The spirits that know
  All mortal consequences, have pronounc'd me thus:
  Fear not Macbeth, no man that's born of woman
  Shall e'er have power upon thee. Then fly false Thanes,
  And mingle with the English epicures;
  The mind I sway by, and the heart I bear,
  Shall never sag with doubt, nor shake with fear.

Enter Servant.

  The Devil damn thee black, thou cream-fac'd loon:
  Where got'st thou that goose look?

SERVANT: There is ten thousand.

MACBETH: Geese villain?

SERVANT: Soldiers sir.

MACBETH: Go prick thy face, and over-red thy fear
  Thou lily-liver'd boy. What soldiers, patch?
  Death of thy soul, those linen cheeks of thine
  Are councillors to fear. What soldiers whey-face?

SERVANT: The English force, so please you.

MACBETH: Take thy face hence.

Exit Servant.

                    Seyton, I am sick at heart,
  When I behold: Seyton, I say, this push
  Will cheer me ever, or disseat me now.
  I have liv'd long enough; my way of life
  Is fall'n into the sear, the yellow leaf,
  And that which should accompany old age,

As honour, love, obedience, troops of friends,
I must not look to have: but in their stead,
Curses, not loud but deep, mouth-honour, breath
Which the poor heart would fain deny, and dare not.
Seyton!

Enter Seyton.

SEYTON: What's your gracious pleasure?

MACBETH: What news more?

SEYTON: All is confirm'd my Lord, which was reported.

MACBETH: I'll fight, till from my bones, my flesh be hack'd.
Give me my armour.

SEYTON: 'Tis not needed yet.

MACBETH: I'll put it on:
Send out moe horses, skirr the country round,
Hang those that talk of fear. Give me mine armour:
How does your patient, doctor?

DOCTOR: Not so sick my Lord,
As she is troubled with thick-coming fancies
That keep her from her rest.

MACBETH: Cure her of that:
Canst thou not minister to a mind diseas'd,
Pluck from the memory a rooted sorrow,
Raze out the written troubles of the brain,
And with some sweet oblivious antidote
Cleanse the stuff'd bosom, of that perilous stuff
Which weighs upon the heart?

DOCTOR: Therein the patient
Must minister to himself.

MACBETH: Throw physic to the dogs, I'll none of it.
Come, put mine armour on: give me my staff:
Seyton, send out: doctor, the Thanes fly from me:
Come sir, dispatch. If thou couldst doctor, cast

The water of my land, find her disease,
And purge it to a sound and pristine health,
I would applaud thee to the very echo,
That should applaud again. Pull 't off I say,
What rhubarb, senna, or what purgative drug
Would scour these English hence: hear'st thou of them?

DOCTOR: Ay my good Lord: your royal preparation
Makes us hear something.

MACBETH: Bring it after me:
I will not be afraid of death and bane,
Till Birnam Forest come to Dunsinane.

DOCTOR: Were I from Dunsinane away, and clear,
Profit again should hardly draw me here.

Exeunt.

V. 4

*Drum and colours. Enter Malcolm, Siward, Macduff, Siward's
son, Mentieth, Caithness, Angus, and Soldiers marching.*

MALCOLM: Cousins, I hope the days are near at hand
That chambers will be safe.

MENTIETH: We doubt it nothing.

SIWARD: What wood is this before us?

MENTIETH: The wood of Birnam.

MALCOLM: Let every soldier hew him down a bough,
And bear't before him, thereby shall we shadow
The numbers of our host, and make discovery
Err in report of us.

SOLDIERS: It shall be done.

SIWARD: We learn no other, but the confident Tyrant
Keeps still in Dunsinane, and will endure
Our setting down before 't.

MALCOLM: 'Tis his main hope:

For where there is advantage to be given,
Both more and less have given him the revolt,
And none serve with him, but constrained things,
Whose hearts are absent too.

MACDUFF: Let our just censures
Attend the true event, and put we on
Industrious soldiership.

SIWARD: The time approaches,
That will with due decision make us know
What we shall say we have, and what we owe:
Thoughts speculative, their unsure hopes relate,
But certain issue, strokes must arbitrate,
Towards which, advance the war.

Exeunt marching.

V. 5

Enter Macbeth, Seyton, and Soldiers, with drum and colours.

MACBETH: Hang out our banners on the outward walls,
The cry is still, they come: our Castle's strength
Will laugh a siege to scorn: here let them lie,
Till famine and the ague eat them up:
Were they not forc'd with those that should be ours,
We might have met them dareful, beard to beard,
And beat them backward home. What is that noise?

A cry within of women.

SEYTON: It is the cry of women, my good Lord.

MACBETH: I have almost forgot the taste of fears:
The time has been, my senses would have cool'd
To hear a night-shriek, and my fell of hair
Would at a dismal treatise rouse, and stir
As life were in't. I have supp'd full with horrors,

Direness familiar to my slaughterous thoughts
Cannot once start me. Wherefore was that cry?
SEYTON: The Queen, my Lord, is dead.
MACBETH: She should have died hereafter;
There would have been a time for such a word:
To-morrow, and to-morrow, and to-morrow,
Creeps in this petty pace from day to day,
To the last syllable of recorded time:
And all our yesterdays, have lighted fools
The way to dusty death. Out, out, brief candle,
Life's but a walking shadow, a poor player,
That struts and frets his hour upon the stage,
And then is heard no more. It is a tale
Told by an idiot, full of sound and fury
Signifying nothing.

Enter a Messenger.

Thou comest to use thy tongue: thy story quickly.
MESSENGER: Gracious my Lord,
I should report that which I say I saw,
But know not how to do it.
MACBETH: Well, say sir.
MESSENGER: As I did stand my watch upon the hill,
I look'd toward Birnam, and anon methought
The Wood began to move.
MACBETH: Liar, and slave.
MESSENGER: Let me endure your wrath, if't be not so:
Within this three mile may you see it coming.
I say, a moving grove.
MACBETH: If thou speak'st false,
Upon the next tree shalt thou hang alive
Till famine cling thee: if thy speech be sooth,
I care not if thou dost for me as much.
I pull in resolution, and begin

To doubt th' equivocation of the fiend,
That lies like truth. Fear not, till Birnam Wood
Do come to Dunsinane; and now a wood
Comes toward Dunsinane. Arm, arm, and out,
If this which he avouches, does appear,
There is nor flying hence, nor tarrying here.
I 'gin to be aweary of the sun,
And wish th' estate o' th' world were now undone.
Ring the alarum-bell, blow wind, come wrack,
At least we'll die with harness on our back.

Exeunt.

V.6

Drums and colours.
Enter Malcolm, Siward, Macduff, and their Army, with boughs.

MALCOLM: Now near enough:
Your leavy screens throw down,
And show like those you are: you, worthy uncle,
Shall with my cousin your right noble son
Lead our first battle. Worthy Macduff, and we
Shall take upon's what else remains to do,
According to our order.

SIWARD: Fare you well:
Do we but find the tyrant's power to-night,
Let us be beaten, if we cannot fight.

MACDUFF: Make all our trumpets speak, give them all
breath,
Those clamorous harbingers of blood, and death.

Exeunt.
Alarums continued.

V.7

Enter Macbeth.

MACBETH: They have tied me to a stake, I cannot fly,
But bear-like I must fight the course. What's he
That was not born of woman? Such a one
Am I to fear, or none.

Enter young Siward.

YOUNG SIWARD: What is thy name?

MACBETH: Thou'lt be afraid to hear it.

YOUNG SIWARD: No: though thou call'st thyself a hotter name
Than any is in hell.

MACBETH: My name's Macbeth.

YOUNG SIWARD: The devil himself could not pronounce a title
More hateful to mine ear.

MACBETH: No: nor more fearful.

YOUNG SIWARD: Thou liest abhorred Tyrant, with my sword
I'll prove the lie thou speak'st.

Fight, and young Siward slain.

MACBETH: Thou wast born of woman:
But swords I smile at, weapons laugh to scorn,
Brandish'd by man that's of a woman born.

Exit.

Alarums. Enter Macduff.

MACDUFF: That way the noise is: Tyrant show thy face;
If thou be'st slain, and with no stroke of mine,
My wife and children's ghosts will haunt me still:
I cannot strike at wretched kerns, whose arms

Are hir'd to bear their staves; either thou Macbeth,
Or else my sword with an unbatter'd edge
I sheathe again undeeded. There thou shouldst be,
By this great clatter, one of greatest note
Seems bruited. Let me find him Fortune,
And more I beg not.

Exit. Alarums.

Enter Malcolm and Siward.

SIWARD: This way my Lord, the Castle's gently render'd:
The Tyrant's people, on both sides do fight,
The noble Thanes do bravely in the war,
The day almost itself professes yours,
And little is to do.

MALCOLM: We have met with foes
That strike beside us.

SIWARD: Enter Sir, the Castle.

Exeunt. Alarum.

Enter Macbeth.

MACBETH: Why should I play the Roman fool, and die
On mine own sword? whiles I see lives, the gashes
Do better upon them.

Enter Macduff.

MACDUFF: Turn hell-hound, turn.

MACBETH: Of all men else I have avoided thee:
But get thee back, my soul is too much charg'd
With blood of thine already.

MACDUFF: I have no words,
My voice is in my sword, thou bloodier villain
Than terms can give thee out.

Fight. Alarum.

MACBETH: Thou losest labour;

As easy mayst thou the intrenchant air
With thy keen sword impress, as make me bleed:
Let fall thy blade on vulnerable crests,
I bear a charmed life, which must not yield
To one of woman born.

MACDUFF: Despair thy charm,
And let the Angel whom thou still hast serv'd
Tell thee, Macduff was from his mother's womb
Untimely ripp'd.

MACBETH: Accursed be that tongue that tells me so;
For it hath cow'd my better part of man:
And be these juggling fiends no more believ'd,
That palter with us in a double sense,
That keep the word of promise to our ear,
And break it to our hope. I'll not fight with thee.

MACDUFF: Then yield thee coward,
And live to be the show, and gaze o' th' time.
We'll have thee, as our rarer monsters are,
Painted upon a pole, and underwrit,
Here may you see the tyrant.

MACBETH: I will not yield
To kiss the ground before young Malcolm's feet,
And to be baited with the rabble's curse.
Though Birnam Wood be come to Dunsinane,
And thou oppos'd, being of no woman born,
Yet I will try the last. Before my body,
I throw my warlike shield: lay on Macduff,
And damn'd be him, that first cries hold, enough.

Exeunt fighting. Alarums.

*Retreat and flourish. Enter with drum and colours, Malcolm,
Siward, Ross, Thanes, and Soldiers.*

MALCOLM: I would the friends we miss, were safe arriv'd.

SIWARD: Some must go off: and yet by these I see,

So great a day as this is cheaply bought.

MALCOLM: Macduff is missing, and your noble son.

ROSS: Your son my Lord, has paid a soldier's debt;
He only liv'd but till he was a man,
The which no sooner had his prowess confirm'd
In the unshrinking station where he fought,
But like a man he died.

SIWARD: Then he is dead?

ROSS: Ay, and brought off the field: your cause of sorrow
Must not be measur'd by his worth, for then
It hath no end.

SIWARD: Had he his hurts before?

ROSS: Ay, on the front.

SIWARD: Why then, God's soldier be he:
Had as I as many sons, as I have hairs,
I would not wish them to a fairer death:
And so his knell is knoll'd.

MALCOLM: He's worth more sorrow,
And that I'll spend for him.

SIWARD: He's worth no more,
They say he parted well, and paid his score,
And so God be with him. Here comes newer comfort.
            Enter Macduff with Macbeth's head.

MACDUFF: Hail King, for so thou art.
Behold where stands
The usurper's cursed head: the time is free:
I see thee compass'd with thy Kingdom's pearl,
That speak my salutation in their minds:
Whose voices I desire aloud with mine.
Hail King of Scotland.

ALL: Hail King of Scotland.
                    Flourish.

MALCOLM: We shall not spend a large expense of time,

Before we reckon with your several loves,
And make us even with you. My Thanes and kinsmen
Henceforth be Earls, the first that ever Scotland
In such an honour nam'd. What's more to do,
Which would be planted newly with the time,
As calling home our exil'd friends abroad,
That fled the snares of watchful tyranny,
Producing forth the cruel ministers
Of this dead butcher, and his fiend-like Queen,
Who (as 'tis thought) by self and violent hands,
Took off her life. This, and what needful else
That calls upon us, by the grace of Grace,
We will perform in measure, time, and place:
So thanks to all at once, and to each one,
Whom we invite, to see us crown'd at Scone.
                    Flourish. Exeunt omnes.

NOTES

References are to the page and line of this edition;
there are 33 lines to the full page.

P. 25 L. 11   *Graymalkin:* a common name for the cat. Cats, paddocks (i.e. toads), hedgehogs, and sometimes chickens, were the witch's familiar spirits. For an old woman to have a pet cat or toad was thought very suspicious.

P. 25 L. 27   *Doubtful it stood ... :* This speech, indeed the whole scene, is unlike Shakespeare's usual style. See Introduction, p. 17.

P. 26 L. 1–2   *Swimmers ... art:* i.e. prevent each other from swimming.

P. 26 L. 6   *kerns and gallowglasses:* (spelt in the Folio 'gallow-grosses') types of wild Irish soldiery, the kern fighting on foot, the gallowglass on horseback, being armed with an axe. Both kinds were unpleasantly familiar to those who had served in Ireland during the campaigns of 1597–1603.

P. 26 L. 7   *quarry:* often emended to *quarrel:* If 'quarry' is the correct reading, its meaning is 'prey': it is used of the beasts slain after a hunt.

P. 26 L. 15   *unseam'd ... chops:* slit him open from belly to cheeks.

P. 26 L. 18   *As whence the sun ... :* as storms follow a fair sunrise. 'Break' has been supplied by editors in place of some missing word.

P. 26 L. 24   *surveying vantage:* seeing an opportunity.

P. 26 L. 25   *furbish'd:* polished, i.e. not stained in battle.

P. 27 L. 1   *memorize another Golgotha:* cause a slaughter which would make the place as memorable as Golgotha (i.e. 'the place of a skull where Christ was crucified').

P. 27 L. 19   *Bellona's bridegroom ... self-comparisons:* 'Macbeth,

a fit mate to the Goddess of War, covered in
armour, showed that he was as good a man as
himself.'

Enter the three Witches: The Witches are not entirely   P. 28 L. 6
consistent. In Holinshed, and in the play when
Macbeth and Banquo later speak of them, the three
Witches are Weird Sisters, creatures of Destiny.
When present, they behave like the malicious, ugly,
old women of contemporary pamphlets describing
the trials of witches. They overlook swine; they
bring wasting diseases on those whom they dislike;
and they indulge in noisome incantations. Belief in
the powers of witches was far from universal in
Shakespeare's day. Reginald Scot in his *Discovery
of Witchcraft* (1584) was boisterously sceptical, and
King James's famous treatise of *Daemonology* (1597)
was written to warn sceptics of the dangers of
incredulity. King James, however, had some reason
for his fervour, for in 1591 a conspiracy of witches
had been discovered in Scotland who plotted to
murder him. One of the witches confessed that she,
with two hundred others, had gone to sea, each in a
sieve, to North Berwick. The meeting of Macbeth
and Banquo with the three Witches is illustrated by
a woodcut in Holinshed, which shows two stout
and elderly Elizabethan gentlemen on horses confronted by three buxom, but sourfaced, women,
amply clad.

Aroint thee: Be off! In witch trials the witch was   P. 28 L. 13
often accused of bewitching her victim because she
had first been refused some request for food or
scraps.

rump-fed ronyon: Editors are not agreed whether   P. 28 L. 13
'rump-fed' means fed on the best, or on the scraps.
Ronyon: scabby creature.

the Tiger. A number of Elizabethan ships were called   P. 28 L. 14
Tiger: probably Shakespeare had in mind Sir Ed-
ward Michelbourne's *Tiger* which returned to
England on 9th July, 1606, after an adventurous

voyage to the East Indies and China, which is related in *Purchas His Pilgrims* [Hakluyt Society, ii, 347.]

P. 28 L. 18   *I'll give thee a wind:* Witches were credited with power over the wind. The tempests which harassed King James when he went to Denmark to fetch his bride were attributed to witchcraft.

P. 29 L. 10   *Weird Sisters:* (spelt 'wayward' and 'weyard' in the Folio) having to do with Destiny.

P. 29 L. 18   *Forres:* correction for Folio 'Soris'.

P. 29 L. 18   *What are these ...:* Shakespeare was sparing in his use of stage directions, but he frequently reveals in the dialogue both the action and the appearance of his characters. For an old woman to be bearded was in itself sinister. When Falstaff (in the *Merry Wives of Windsor*) escapes disguised as a witch, Parson Evans comments 'By yea and no, I think the 'oman is a witch indeed: I like not when a 'oman has a great peard'.

P. 31 L. 5   *insane root:* hemlock or henbane, supposed to cause madness.

P. 31 L. 20   *As thick as tale:* i.e. as fast as the tale could be told, fresh news came. 'Tale' is sometimes unnecessarily altered to 'hail'.

P. 31 L. 21   *post with post:* In Shakespeare's time communication between the Court and the important towns and ports was by means of post horses. At each stage on the main roads, a supply of horses was kept always ready, and letters passed to and fro with surprising speed. The sight of the post boy blowing his horn, as he galloped along roads and through towns, evoked many poetic images for speed.

P. 32 L. 12   *behind:* Yet to come.

P. 32 L. 25   *Swelling Act ... throne:* powerful scene when I shall become King.

P. 32 L. 27   *This supernatural soliciting ... but what is not:* This speech is the first indication of Macbeth's towering imagination which later will project visibly before him the dagger, and the phantom of Banquo. The thought of murder becomes so vivid a picture of Duncan murdered, that it produces bodily terror. When in the grip of his imagination, Macbeth is oblivious to everything; as Banquo observes, 'Look how our partner's rapt'.

fantastical: existing only in the fantasy or imagination.   P. 33 L. 3

single state of man: Man was often regarded as a microcosm, a universe in miniature, with all the functions of a kingdom existing in himself. *State*: kingdom.   P. 33 L. 4

function is smother'd in surmise: action is choked by imagination.   P. 33 L. 5

runs through: comes to the end of.   P. 33 L. 15

those in commission: For important state trials the accused was tried not by the ordinary judges but by a body of great persons summoned by a special commission.   P. 34 L. 5

no art ... face: there is no known way of reading a man's character from his face.   P. 34 L. 16

The rest ... you: i.e. anything done for you is a pleasure.   P. 35 L. 24

the harbinger: an official of the Court whose duty was to make preparations for provision and lodging when the Sovereign went on progress.   P. 35 L. 25

dues of rejoicing: i.e. joy.   P. 36 L. 20

compunctious visitings of Nature: natural feelings of pity.   P. 37 L. 31

murthr'ing ministers: spirits of murder.   P. 38 L. 1

sovereign sway: absolute power.   P. 38 L. 28

To alter favour: to change countenance.   P. 38 L. 31

martlet: (emendation for Folio 'bartlet'), martin.   P. 39 L. 8

procreant cradle: nest where the young are hatched.   P. 39 L. 12

God 'ild: God reward.   P. 39 L. 19

poor ... contend: poor and weak in comparison.   P. 39 L. 23

P. 39 L. 27   *rest your hermits*: i.e. are bound to pray for you.

P. 40 L. 18   *trammel up*: 'if only the murder could have no after
effects but be final and successful at Duncan's death.'
Trammel up is used, either of hobbling a horse, or of
enveloping in a net.

P. 40 L. 21   *school*: sometimes emended to *shoal*. 'School' is
the older form of the word, still surviving in such
a phrase as 'a school of porpoises'.

P. 41 L. 29   *Art thou afear'd*: the irresistible taunt to a soldier of
Macbeth's reputation.

P. 41 L. 32   *ornament of life*: i.e. the crown.

P. 42 L. 2   *adage*: proverb. It is common in several languages.
In Heywood's *Proverbs* (1566) it runs – 'The cat
would eat fish, and would not wet her feet.'

P. 42 L. 26   *memory ... a fume ... limbeck only*: memory shall
be confused by the fumes of drink and the brain be
but a still distilling confused thoughts.

ACT TWO   The divisions into Acts and Scenes though made in
the Folio are not always apt. There is no pause in
the action from I. vii to the end of II iii. The play
is constructed in three phases. (1) The murder of
Duncan (I. i. to II. iv.) (2) The murder of Banquo
(III. i–vi.) (3) The Retribution (IV. i. to end).

P. 43 L. 24   *heavy summons*: excessive sleepiness.

P. 44 L. 6   *shut up ... content*: he has ended the day supremely
happy.

P. 44 L. 7   *Being ... wrought*: i.e. as we were not prepared our
entertainment was not as lavish as it would otherwise
have been.

P. 44 L. 23   *bosom franchised ... clear*: i.e. my heart free and
loyalty untainted. In the *Chronicle* Banquo is said to
have been a fellow conspirator with Macbeth against
Duncan. Since, however, he was the reputed ancestor
of King James I, Shakespeare is careful to acquit him
of such treachery.

P. 46 L. 7   *fatal bellman ... stern'st good night*: The night before

an execution in London the great bell of St. Sepul-
chre's Church was tolled, and at midnight the bellman rang a handbell outside the condemned cell,
and called on the condemned to remember their
sins. This custom was but newly established, the
endowment having been given by Robert Dow,
Merchant Taylor, in 1604.

charge: i.e. that which is entrusted to their keeping. **P. 46 L. 9**

hangman's hands: to Shakespeare's audience, fresh **P. 47 L. 9**
from the excitement of the execution of the plotters
in the Powder Treason, this image would be full of
vivid and ghastly significance. It was the hangman's
business to tear the vitals out of his victim before
hacking him into pieces.

Methought ... Sleep no more: There is intense irony **P. 47 L. 17**
in these mutterings of Macbeth, for they echo the
sentiments of Sidney and other writers of love
sonnets on Sleep, e.g.

Come Sleep, O Sleep, the certain knot of peace,
The bathing place of wits, the balm of woe,
The poor man's wealth, the prisoner's release,
The indifferent judge between the high and low.
      (*Astrophel and Stella*, xxxix, ed.1591.)

ravell'd sleave: tangled skein.   **P. 47 L. 19**

gild ... guilt: a common pun. Shakespeare's con- **P. 48 L. 9**
temporaries were not very exact in their sense of
colour; 'gold' and 'red' were regarded as one colour.

A little water clears us of this deed: In *Macbeth* three **P. 48 L. 26**
images constantly recur – Blood, Water, Darkness:
the three ideas hereafter become an obsession of
Macbeth and his wife. Her light words 'a little
water' are the ironic comment on Macbeth's
knowledge that henceforward 'all great Neptune's
Ocean' will never wash away the blood from the
murderer's hands.

Enter a Porter: Coleridge disliked this drunken **P. 49 L. 8**
Porter and thought that the speech was written to
please the mob. Actually it is magnificent drama,

for the sense of horror, culminating after the murder,
must be released, and a complete change of mood
allows the audience to relieve their emotions in
laughter. Moreover the jesting of the Porter is ironic
and relevant, for he pretends to be the Porter of
Hell, without realising that he is so indeed.

P. 49 L. 12   *Here's a farmer, that hang'd himself on th' expectation
of plenty:* The greediness of farmers, who hoarded
corn in the hope of dearth, was a common subject
for jest and satire. In Jonson's *Every Man out of his
Humour* (1600) Sordido the farmer hangs himself
when his hopes are disappointed, and then, when he
is rescued by his neighbours, abuses them for cutting,
and not untying, the rope.

P. 49 L. 16   *Faith here's an equivocator ... equivocate to Heaven:*
The doctrine of equivocation, which was regarded as
being practised particularly by the Jesuits, had been
much discussed during the religious troubles of the
ten years preceding the Gunpowder Plot, and at the
Trial of Father Garnet on 28th March 1606 equivocation was a major issue. Coke, the Attorney General,
who was always a bullying and unfair advocate, in
his speech for the prosecution attacked Garnet with
great bitterness. 'For dissimulation,' he remarked,
'there is a Tratise of Equivocation, seen and allowed
by Garnet, and by Blackwell, the arch-priest;
wherein it is maintained, under the pretext of a mixt
proposition (that is, compounded of a natural and
vocal proposition) that it is lawful and justifiable to
express one part of a man's mind, and retain another.
By this doctrine people are indeed taught, not only
simple lying, but fearful and damnable blasphemy.
Garnet and the Jesuits also maintain, that it is lawful
to equivocate when examined by a judge, who hath
not lawful authority to examine.' At Garnet's execution on May 3rd, the Recorder 'wished him not to
deceive himself, nor beguile his own soul, he was
come to die, and must die; requiring him not to
equivocate with his last breath, if he knew anything
that might be a danger to the King or State, he

should now declare it. Garnet said, "It is no time now to equivocate": how it was lawful, and when, he had shewed his mind elsewhere. But saith he, "I do not now equivocate, and more than I have confessed, I do not know." ' (*A true and perfect relation of the whole proceedings against ... Garnet, a Jesuit, and his confederates.* 1606.)

stealing out of a French hose: French hose (breeches) P. 49 L. 21
were particularly large and baggy so that the tailor could easily purloin part of the cloth.

dire combustion: some terrible event about to blaze P. 51 L. 11
out.

Gorgon: the snake-headed monster Medusa, so ter- P. 51 L. 30
rible to look upon that a glance turned the beholder to stone.

To countenance this horror: i.e. to give a suitable P. 52 L. 6
accompaniment to this horror you must stalk on like evil spirits. This, and Macbeth's other speeches for the rest of this scene abound in farfetched metaphors revealing his overacted horror.

lac'd with his golden blood: overlaid as with the lace P. 53 L. 16
sewn on to a garment. Gold lace was often used to ornament the fashionable man's clothes. For 'golden' see note on p. 48 l. 9.

fate, hid in an auger-hole: destruction may be hidden P. 53 L. 28
in any little circumstance.

naked frailties ... exposure: i.e. when we have put P. 54 L. 1
on our clothes, for they have come straight from bed.

travelling lamp: i.e. the sun. P. 55 L. 10

towering in her pride of place: towering proudly aloft. P. 55 L. 16

Colmekill: Iona, the ancient burying place of the P. 56 L. 15
Scottish kings.

My Genius is rebuk'd, as it is said P. 59 L. 5
Mark Antony's was by Caesar: Shakespeare afterwards made an episode of this in *Antony and Cleopatra* (II. iii. 18) where the soothsayer warns Antony to leave Caesar:

Thy demon that thy spirit which keeps thee, is
Noble, courageous, high unmatcheable,
Where Caesar's is not. But near him, thy angel
Becomes a fear, as being o'erpower'd.

P. 59 L. 31   *held ... fortune:* was responsible for your bad fortune.

P. 60 L. 1   *Pass'd in probation:* when I gave you the proofs.

P. 60 L. 2   *borne in hand:* deceived.

P. 60 L. 13   *so gospell'd:* such a true Christian.

P. 60 L. 21   *valued file:* the list of those valued.

P. 61 L. 29   *Acquaint you with the perfect spy o' th' time:* send
someone to tell you the exact moment.

P. 61 L. 33   *rubs:* one of Shakespeare's frequent images from
bowling. A 'rub' is an unevenness in the green
which turns the course of the bowl.

P. 62 L. 30   *scorch'd the snake:* often emended to 'scotch'd', but
to anyone who has seen a snake moribund after a
grass fire the image is apt.

P. 63 L. 3   *But let the frame ... in fear:* 'rather than continue in
this state of fear, we will break down the whole
fabric of the Universe, and let heaven and earth
suffer for it.'

P. 63 L. 29   *Nature's copy's not eterne:* Man holds life of Nature
by lease, which is temporary only. *Copy:* lease.

P. 64 L. 5   *come, seeling Night:* When hawks were tamed a
thread was passed through their eyelids which were
thus 'seeled' until they were used to the hood.

P. 64 L. 18   *Enter three Murtherers:* The presence of the third
murderer is not explained.

P. 65 L. 3   *within the note of expectation:* noted as expected at
the feast.

P. 65 L. 29   *You know your own degrees ... Our hostess keeps her*
– P. 66 L. 4   *state:* In this state banquet, the guests sit according
to their rank while Lady Macbeth sits apart en-
throned on a chair of state. The stately beginning of
of the feast contrasts with its abrupt and uncere-
monious ending.

Notes

large in mirth : unrestrained in your enjoyment. P. 66 L. 13

the feast is sold ... without it. : 'there is no hospitality P. 67 L. 7
at a feast where the guests are not made welcome :
without ceremony it is a mere bought meal ; one can
feed better at home ; away from home (*From thence*),
ceremony should accompany the feast.'

extend his passion : increase his emotion. P. 68 L. 6

our monuments Shall be the maws of kites : our graves P. 68 L. 23
shall be in the mouths of birds of prey.

desert : i.e. a place whence there is no escape. P. 69 L. 31

Stand not upon the order of your going : do not wait to P. 70 L. 18
take leave in order of precedence.

understood relations : the relation between the omen P. 70 L. 27
and its meaning.

What is the night? : This abrupt change in the P. 70 L. 29
dialogue seems to indicate a cut in the play.

season ... sleep : sleep which gives seasoning to keep P. 71 L. 13
fresh.

initiate fear : the novice's fear ; i.e. when I am more P. 71 L. 16
experienced in murder, I shall cease to be nervous.

Enter the three Witches, meeting Hecat : The whole of P. 71 L. 20
this scene, and Act IV Scene I, is probably not by
Shakespeare.

artificial sprites : spirits created by magic art. P. 72 L. 17

Song within 'Come away, come away'. The complete P. 72 L. 27
song is to be found in Middleton's *Witch*.

the most pious. Edward : Edward the Confessor. P. 73 L. 31

free honours : honours bestowed on free men. P. 74 L. 9

Witch's mummy : dried corpse of a witch. Mummy P. 75 L. 21
from Egypt was formerly considered a valuable drug.

Song : 'Black Spirits,' &c. : also found in full in P. 76 L. 10
Middleton's *Witch*.

Nature's germen : the seeds of matter, all living things. P. 76 L. 28

take a bond of Fate : i.e. to enforce the agreement with P. 78 L. 1
Fate, he will kill Macduff.

P. 78 L. 18   *impress the forest :* to impress, or imprest, is to con-
script soldiers. One cannot, says Macbeth, turn the
trees into soldiers and make them march.

P. 79 L. 4   *A show of eight Kings :* i.e. a dumb show, or procession
of silent figures.

P. 79 L. 15   *That two-fold balls, and treble sceptres carry :* i.e. the
regalia of the United Kingdoms of England,
Scotland and Ireland.

P. 80 L. 14   *The flighty purpose … my hand :* 'the plan is never
fulfilled unless carried out at once.'

P. 81 L. 28   *But float … and move :* like a ship, powerless in a
tempest, carried hither and thither.

P. 84 L. 11   *Act IV, Scene 3 :* The conversation between Malcolm
and Macduff is closely taken from Holinshed.

P. 85 L. 4   *virtuous nature … imperial charge :* 'even a good man
may do a vile deed if ordered by a King.'

P. 89 L. 18   *'Tis call'd the Evil :* Holinshed notes that Edward the
Confessor 'used to help those that were vexed with
the disease, commonly called the King's Evil
[*scrofula*], and left that virtue as it were a portion of
inheritance unto his successors.' The reference to
the power is rather dragged in to compliment King
James I, who at first was unwilling to continue the
practice until urged by his English ministers. In 1617
he is recorded to have healed 53 persons at one time
at Lincoln. The succeeding Stuart sovereigns continued the practice, down to Queen Anne, who
'touched' Dr. Johnson, as a child, but without
success.

P. 90 L. 13   *modern ecstasy :* slight mental disturbance.

P. 91 L. 13   *fee-grief … single breast :* a grief that has a single
owner.

P. 92 L. 6   *He has no children :* Either, Malcolm has no children
and so cannot fully feel Macduff's sorrow, or, since
Macbeth has no children, Macduff cannot hope for
a complete revenge.

What will these hands ne'er be clean?: This is the last P. 94 L. 15
echo of 'A little water clears us of this deed.'

mortal consequences: human fate.   P. 97 L. 7

epicures: gluttons, and so no soldiers.   P. 97 L. 10

Devil ... black: black was the Devil's own colour, P. 97 L. 14
and it was believed that when the Devil claimed a
soul the body turned black.

my way of life: Dr. Johnson wished to read 'May of P. 97 L. 29
life': he was probably right: a misreading of 'w'
for 'm' is common. The image of May for youth at
its prime is frequent, as in *Astrophel and Stella* XXI:
  If now the May of my years much decline,
  What can be hop'd my harvest time will be.

cast The water of my land: Inspection of the urine as P. 98 L. 33
an aid to diagnosis was the common practice of
contemporary physicians.

chambers will be safe: a man's private life will be safe. P. 99 L. 19

Let ... event: let us wait till after the battle before P. 100 L. 5
passing judgment.

thoughts speculative ... relate: i.e. these guesses (about P. 100 L. 11
the loyalty of Macbeth's soldiers) are mere hopes.

Hang out our banners ... they come: The text repro- P. 100 L. 17
duces the Folio. Modern editors usually punctuate:
  Hang out our banners on the outward walls;
  The cry is still, 'They come.'
'Still' may, however, be taken as an adjective:
Macbeth, as an experienced soldier, noticing that
the clamour outside has suddenly ceased, realizes
that the enemy are about to assault; hence his order
to man the walls.

forced: reinforced.   P. 100 L. 21

She should have died hereafter: she would have P. 101 L. 4
died at some time or other. In this speech the
personal tragedy of Macbeth culminates. After all
the blood, fury and agony of his life, he comes at
last to the conclusion that life itself is utterly without
meaning.

P. 103 L. 4   *bear-like I must fight the course:* In bear-baiting the bear was tied to a stake and the dogs let in to worry it for a course, or round.

P. 104 L. 19   *play the Roman fool:* commit suicide in the moment of defeat, like Cato or Brutus.

P. 105 L. 29   *Exeunt fighting:* After the stage direction the Folio adds *Enter fighting, and Macbeth slain.* There has clearly been some revision in this scene.

P. 106 L. 6   *unshrinking station:* by standing fast where he stood.

P. 106 L. 23   *Enter Macduff with Macbeth's head:* Severed heads were often used as properties in the Elizabethan playhouse. In the inventory of the properties of the Admiral's Players in 1598 one item was 'old Mahomet's head'.

P. 106 L. 27   *compass'd with thy Kingdom's pearl:* surrounded by the pearl (or as the modern expression has it, the 'flower') of the kingdom.

GLOSSARY

addition: a title of honour added to the name, so 'honour'

address'd: made ready

admir'd: wondered at

affeer'd: confirmed

all-thing: in every way

anon: 'I am coming'

annoyance: harm

antic: fantastic

approve: demonstrate

assay: effort

avouch: proclaim

badg'd: lit. wearing a badge of blood

bane: destruction

bare-fac'd: without concealment

battle: division (of an army)

beguile: deceive

beldams: ugly old women

benison: blessing

blood-bolter'd: matted with blood

bodements: prophecies

borne: managed

botches: flaws

break: reveal

breech'd: covered as with breeches

brinded: branded, striped

bruited: noised abroad

cabin'd: confined in a small room

card: the card marking the points of the compass

casing: enclosing

cast: throw up

charg'd: burdened

chaudron: entrails

choppy: chapped

chough: jackdaw

clear: innocent

clearness: freedom from suspicion

clept: called

cling: wither

closet: chest, used for private papers

coign of vantage: convenient corner

composition: agreement, terms of peace

compt: account, which must be produced at the audit

consent: party

continent: containing, restraining

convince: overpower

corporal: bodily

cours'd: pursued

coz: cousin, kinsman

cracks: cannon-balls

crests: heads

cribb'd: confined in a crib

cross'd: thwarted

dear: heartfelt

demi-wolves: half-dog, half-wolf

dispute : strive against
distance : hate
doubt : suspect
Doom : doomsday
dudgeon : handle

earnest : a token payment on account of the main sum due
ecstasy : madness, any strong emotion
expedition : haste

faculties : powers
fantastical : existing only in the fantasy, a creation of the imagination
farrow : litter
favour : face
fell : skin
file : list
fil'd : defiled
flaw : gust of wind
flighty : fleet
forbid : accursed
foisons : abundance
franchis'd : free
furbish'd : newly made ready

gall : bitterness
get : beget
grac'd : full of grace
gulf : stomach

harness : armour
Harpier : a familiar spirit
Hecat : so spelt (and pronounced) in the Folio, one of the goddesses in the underworld
hie : hasten

house-keeper : watch-dog
hurly-burly : confusion
husbandry : confusion
Hyrcan : Caspian

incarnadine : make red
initiate : belonging to a novice
interdiction : exclusion
intermission : interval
intrenchant : that cannot be cut
invention : falsehood

jump : risk
jutty frieze : projection on a building

largess : gift of money
latch : catch
lated : belated
lighted : newly come to earth
lily-liver'd : cowardly
limited : allotted
line : aid
lodg'd : (of corn) laid flat
luxurious : vicious

magot-pies : magpies
mansionry : home
mated : confounded
maw : jaw
measure : quantity of drink, so 'toast'
metaphysical : supernatural
mettle : the same word as 'metal', hard substance, iron disposition
minion : darling
missives : messengers
moe : more
mortified : dead

nave: navel
nice: fastidious
nightgown: dressing-gown
nonpareil: without a parallel

oblivious: causing forgetfulness
obscure bird: the owl
offices: (1) servants' quarters
  (2) duties
old: slang for 'any amount of'
overcome: overshadow
owe: own

palpable: perceptible by the
  senses
patch: fool
pauser: that which restrains
peak: waste away
pent-house: a lean-to shed, so
  'pent-house' lid = eyelid
pester'd: troubled
physics pain: cures trouble
posset: hot drink, made of
  wine or ale and milk
posters: travelling post-haste
power: army
present: immediate
pretence: plot, design
proof: armour
purveyor: fore-runner

quarry: heap of slain after a
  hunt
quell: murder

rapt: entranced
ravin: prey on
rawness: haste
register'd: recorded

remorse: pity
roof'd: under the roof, present
rooky: murky
round: dance
rugged: rough

scarf up: blindfold
seated: fixed
security: false sense of safety
self-abuse: self-deception
sensible: perceived by the
  senses
sere: dry
sewer: server
shaft: arrow
shard-borne: carried on its
  shiny wings
shough: shaggy-haired dog
sightless: invisible
skipping: nimble
skirr: scour
slab: thick, muddy
sleave: skein of silk
sleek: make smooth
sleights: tricks
sliver'd: torn off
speculation: power of sight
stamp: coin or medal, stamped
  with the King's image
still: always
storehouse: tomb

tending: attendance
Thane: a title corresponding to
  Earl
thralls: serfs
titles: possessions
top: crown
trains: enticements
trenched: gashed
tugg'd with: pulled about by

unlineal: belonging to another descent
unrough: smooth-chinned
utterance: uttermost

virtue: power
vizards: masks
vouch'd: warranted

wassail: carousing
water-rugs: dogs used to the water
weal: commonwealth
wound up: completed

yesty: frothy

PENGUIN POPULAR CLASSICS

Published or forthcoming

PENGUIN POPULAR CLASSICS

Published or forthcoming

Anna Sewell	Black Beauty
Mary Shelley	Frankenstein
Johanna Spyri	Heidi
Robert Louis Stevenson	The Black Arrow
	A Child's Garden of Verses
	Dr Jekyll and Mr Hyde
	Kidnapped
	Treasure Island
Bram Stoker	Dracula
Jonathan Swift	Gulliver's Travels
W. M. Thackeray	Vanity Fair
Leo Tolstoy	War and Peace
Anthony Trollope	Barchester Towers
	Framley Parsonage
	The Small House at Allington
	The Warden
Mark Twain	The Adventures of Huckleberry Finn
	The Adventures of Tom Sawyer
	The Prince and the Pauper
Vatsyayana	The Kama Sutra
Jules Verne	Around the World in Eighty Days
	Journey to the Centre of the Earth
	Twenty Thousand Leagues under the Sea
Voltaire	Candide
Edith Wharton	The Age of Innocence
	Ethan Frome
Oscar Wilde	The Happy Prince and Other Stories
	The Importance of Being Earnest
	Lady Windermere's Fan
	Lord Arthur Savile's Crime
	The Picture of Dorian Gray
	A Woman of No Importance
Virginia Woolf	Mrs Dalloway
	Orlando
	To the Lighthouse

PENGUIN POPULAR POETRY

Published or forthcoming

The Selected Poems *of:*

Matthew Arnold
William Blake
Robert Browning
Robert Burns
Lord Byron
John Donne
Thomas Hardy
John Keats
Rudyard Kipling
Alexander Pope
Alfred Tennyson
William Wordsworth
William Yeats

and collections of:

Seventeenth-Century Poetry
Eighteenth-Century Poetry
Poetry of the Romantics
Victorian Poetry
Twentieth-Century Poetry
Scottish Folk and Fairy Tales